What Will

HARRY Do?

The Unofficial Guide To

PAYOFFS and POSSIBILITIES
in Book 7

by Janet Scott Batchler

ACKNOWLEDGMENTS

A great thank you first and foremost to John Granger (www.HogwartsProfessor.com), author of *Looking for God In Harry Potter* (Tyndale, 2004), who encouraged me to collect these essays into book form.

Most of these essays first appeared in some form on my blog, "Quoth the Maven" (www.quoththemaven.blogspot.com), and I am grateful to the many readers and commenters who pointed out my mistakes, my misdirections, and even my bulls-eyes. Special thanks to frequent and insightful visitors Regina Doman and Sarah Beach. Thanks also to those who linked to my blog, so I could "meet" and hear from so many folks, including in particular Barbara Nicolosi, Travis Prinzi, and LaShawn Barber.

In addition, I am grateful for comments received on various message boards run by John Granger, including the online classes hosted by Barnes and Noble in summer and fall of 2005. Special thanks to Pat, Beth, Trudy, Travis, Helen, and Maureen in particular!

Thanks also to all those who volunteered to help me proofread, and especially to Kale Zelden for stepping in to cast an editor's eye over the final draft.

A huge thank you to cover artist Joseph Rubio (www.rubiomedia.com). What a wonderful job he did, especially when all I gave him to work with was, "I don't know, maybe yellow lettering would be nice."

My deepest gratitude (joined, I am sure, by yours) to J.K. Rowling, for allowing us into her magical world. Each time I read the *Harry Potter* books, I am even more in awe of her imagination and her achievement. I am grateful for the unofficial opportunity to muse on what comes next, and to share those musings with others.

Finally, great thanks to my husband Lee for not laughing as I became, before his eyes, a *Harry Potter* geek, and for appreciating Rowling's genius with me. And thanks to my children, Cory and Sabrina, for also catching the magic, and for allowing me to read all the books out loud to them, not caring that my doing so slowed their own race to the ending.

SPOILER WARNING!!

Every bit of this book -- every chapter, every paragraph, every sentence -- assumes that you have read all six of J.K. Rowling's *Harry Potter* books. If you have not read them all, please rush right out and buy them. (Preferably in hardcover. For full price.) And read them, cover to cover. Only then will it be safe to read forward without having surprises and plot twists ruined for you.

If you have read them all, then please... turn the page and let's get started!

TABLE OF CONTENTS

INTRODUCTION

How lucky we are!

Future generations -- pretty much everyone yet to pick up a *Harry Potter* book -- will read knowing that to know what happens next all they have to do is move on to the next book.

But we live in a glorious limbo. We've read everything from *Harry Potter and the Sorcerer's* (or *Philosopher's*) *Stone* to *Harry Potter and the Half-Blood Prince*... and we <u>don't</u> know what happens next! We get to enjoy all the speculation, all the wild musings, all the "what if's." No one else reading the books will ever get to experience what we're experiencing right now.

So what *will* happen next...?

I'm a screenwriter by trade, not a novelist. And as a screenwriter, my writing lives and breathes only by the power of its set-ups and payoffs. If I want my audience to receive any kind of emotional punch, I have to set it up. Only then will the audience get that wonderful feeling of having their expectations fulfilled. On the flip side, if I've set up a plot point or a relationship moment and I fail to pay it off, fail to provide the audience with what they were anticipating, I've failed in my job.

Not only do I *use* set-ups and payoffs in my daily work, I get to sit around thinking about them, too. Because I don't just write screenplays, I teach how to write them. I teach my students the importance of getting their set-ups and payoffs straight, usually drawing my examples from terrifically-written movies such as *Groundhog Day*, *Aliens*, and *Back to the Future*.

But in 2005, the year *Harry Potter and the Half-Blood Prince* came out, I found myself also referencing *Harry Potter*. Look at the marvelous way Mrs. Figg is referred to as early as Chapter 2 of *Harry Potter and the Sorcerer's Stone* -- with no payoff until she reveals herself as a Squib after the dementors attack Harry and Dudley four whole books later! What masterful plotting! What a wonderful payoff.

Those students who had read the books understood what I was talking about -- and they began to wonder aloud: What *other* set-ups and payoffs were we missing in *Harry Potter*?

And I said to myself, "Gee, someday when I actually have time, I should go through the *Harry Potter* books and actually study the set-ups and payoffs."

Shortly afterward, I found the time. Or made the time.

Now, of course, we can't know all the payoffs without Book 7 in hand. But that's part of what makes it fun. After Book 7 is out, the exercise will just become a final exam question for Children's Lit 101. Now, however, we get to speculate, see what the payoffs *could* be, try to guess which are the real set-ups deserving of payoff, and which, if any, are the red herrings.

Can we know everything about what will happen in Book 7? No. J.K. Rowling is too inventive a writer for us to be able to predict what she will do. But she has been so meticulous in her use of set-ups and payoffs so far, I believe we will see most (if not all) of her dramatic set-ups paid off beautifully in Book 7.

In the meantime, let's have some fun digging in!

CHAPTER 1

SET-UPS, PAYOFFS AND HOW THEY WORK

So what are set-ups and payoffs, anyway? As a well-handled example, let's look at the Vanishing Cabinet.

The Vanishing Cabinet storyline comes to its full fruition, of course, in *Half-Blood Prince* when Draco Malfoy uses it to create a secret passageway into Hogwarts, allowing Death Eaters onto the grounds and ultimately resulting in Dumbledore's death.

If that Vanishing Cabinet had been introduced for the first time in *Half-Blood Prince*, we'd all say, "Hey, wait a minute! That's not fair!" But it wasn't tossed in willy-nilly. It was carefully set up, every step of the way. Let's take a quick look:

In *Chamber of Secrets*: First the Cabinet is introduced in Borgin and Burkes:

> *Harry looked quickly around and spotted a large black*
> *cabinet to his left; he shot inside it and pulled the doors closed,*
> *leaving a small crack to peer through.* [CS-4]

Had he closed the door completely, would he have been sent magically to the other Vanishing Cabinet? Perhaps. (But, as some have cleverly pointed out, clearly Harry had read *The Lion, The Witch and the Wardrobe* and learned that one should never close a cabinet door completely behind oneself.)

Next, we meet the Cabinet's mate at Hogwarts:

> *As Filch lowered his quill, there was a great BANG! on the ceiling of the office, which made the oil lamp rattle.... Harry didn't much like Peeves, but couldn't help feeling grateful for his timing. Hopefully, whatever Peeves had done (and it sounded as though he'd wrecked something very big this time) would distract Filch from Harry....*

> *Filch was looking triumphant. "That vanishing cabinet was extremely valuable!" he was saying gleefully to Mrs. Norris. "We'll have Peeves out this time, my sweet--"* [CS-8, excerpted]

We don't really notice the reference to the Vanishing Cabinet, because we're more interested at the revelation that Filch is a Squib. But the reference is there. And more: Not only do we know the Cabinet exists, we know it's broken.

Onward to *Order of the Phoenix*:

> *"Yeah, Montague tried to do us during break," said George.*

> *"What do you mean, 'tried'?" said Ron quickly.*

> *"He never managed to get all the words out," said Fred, "due to the fact that we forced him headfirst into that Vanishing Cabinet on the first floor."* [OP-28]

The fact that Montague stays "vanished" for quite some time shows that the Cabinet still works, and it lets us know what it does.

Now on to *Half-Blood Prince*: We learn first that the Cabinet's mate is still at Borgin and Burkes, in a throwaway of a line that could just be adding color:

*There in the midst of the cases full of skulls and old bottles
stood Draco Malfoy with his back to them, just visible beyond the
very same large black cabinet in which Harry had once hidden to
avoid Malfoy and his father.* [HBP-6]

We next run in to the Vanishing Cabinet (which has now
acquired capital-letter status) when Harry enters the Room of
Requirement looking for a place to hide his Potions book:

*Harry hurried forward into one of the many alleyways
between all this hidden treasure. He turned right past an
enormous stuffed troll, ran on a short way, took a left at the
broken Vanishing Cabinet in which Montague had got lost the
previous year, finally pausing beside a large cupboard that seemed
to have had acid thrown at its blistered surface.* [HBP-24]

Harry doesn't realize the significance of the cabinet, doesn't
realize it's what he's been looking for all along -- and neither do we.
But the set-up is there.

We've now had set-up after set-up, all subtly handled. And the
payoff comes at the end of *Half-Blood Prince*.

In response to a question about how he managed to smuggle
Death Eaters into Hogwarts, Draco Malfoy tells Dumbledore:

*"I had to mend that broken Vanishing Cabinet that no one's
used for years. The one Montague got lost in last year."*

*"Aaaah." Dumbledore's sigh was half a groan. He closed
his eyes for a moment. "That was clever.... There is a pair, I
take it?"*

*"In Borgin and Burkes," said Malfoy, "and they make a
kind of passage between them. Montague told me that when he*

was stuck in the Hogwarts one, he was trapped in limbo but sometimes he could hear what was going on at school, and sometimes what was going on in the shop, as if the cabinet was traveling between them, but he couldn't make anyone hear him.... Everyone thought it was a really good story, but I was the only one who realized what it meant -- even Borgin didn't know -- I was the one who realized there could be a way into Hogwarts through the cabinets if I fixed the broken one." [HBP-27]

We had set-up after set-up, most of them tossed off casually -- and we didn't realize what they meant at the time. But when Draco explains, we can't complain we weren't warned, because all the set-ups were there.

One more example of how set-ups and payoffs work in Chapter 2, then let's take a look at the other treats J.K. Rowling has set up for us, all to make Book 7 as satisfying and exciting as possible.

CHAPTER 2

LOVE POTIONS

Another exquisite example of set-up and payoff structure is the use of love potions through *Half-Blood Prince*. Started and completed in one book, this is a marvelously tight example of how we move from set-up to payoff to *unexpected* payoff.

We're introduced to Love Potions at Weasley's Wizard Wheezes, where Fred and George are doing a brisk business in "Wonder Witch" products [HBP-6]. Note how deftly the set-up is tossed off: We learn Fred and George are selling love potions, they assure us the potions work, and then we swoop off sideways to what we think is the *real* meat of that scenelet, a discussion of all the boys with their tongues hanging out over Ginny.

We learn more about Love Potions in our first class with Slughorn:

> *"Amortentia doesn't really create love, of course. It is impossible to manufacture or imitate love. No, this will simply cause a powerful infatuation or obsession. It is probably the most dangerous and powerful potion in this room -- oh yes,"* [Slughorn] said, nodding gravely at Malfoy and Nott, both of whom were smirking skeptically. *"When you have seen as much of life as I have, you will not underestimate the power of obsessive love..."* [HBP-9]

Note how much this scene gives us. We get more introduction to Slughorn's character -- Can anyone imagine *Snape* teaching how to brew love potions?! We get a hint that Hermione is indeed at least a bit in love, since she declines to say what she smells in the love potion (What could it be -- Ron's stinky sweat socks?).

We also get two important set-ups: One for the Romilda-tries-to-trick-Harry storyline... and one that explains much of what we will learn about Tom Riddle. All tossed off in, again, what seems like a character-based moment, not a plot point.

Perhaps Slughorn seems to wax a tad romantic in saying that Amortentia is the "most dangerous" potion in the room. But as it turns out, he is exactly on target.

For we learn very soon after this scene how Merope used a love potion to trap Tom Riddle, Sr. into a sham of a marriage [HBP-10].

"Most dangerous" potion, indeed! For without it, Lord Voldemort would never have been born!

That's a payoff to one of our set-ups. But we still have to pay off all those love potions lining the twins' shelves. We get that payoff when Romilda Vane tries to slip Harry chocolates full of love potion [HBP-15]. Our set-up here takes an unexpected twist, however, when it's not Harry who eats the love potion, but Ron [HBP-18].

Suddenly we have two strings of set-ups colliding. Harry drags Ron to Slughorn for help, Slughorn whips up an antidote, they all celebrate with a little oak-matured mead -- and Ron almost dies of the poisoned mead, causing Harry to search frantically for a bezoar.

With one little set-up, all of a sudden we are (a) reminded of that ever-so-important first Potions class with Snape; (b) warned yet again that the security of Hogwarts has been breached; (c) sent down the path (whether it be true or false) of suspecting Slughorn's loyalties; and (d) handed a blatant hint toward the ultimate unraveling of the book's plot:

> *"[Slughorn] could be under the Imperius Curse," said George.* [HBP-19]

What masterful plotting and spinning indeed, to pull all this together with what was really a little throwaway moment! I expect much of Book 7 will be like this: We will get to watch in amazement as all the puzzle pieces (some of which we didn't even realize *were* pieces of the puzzle) fall together.

Will we see Love Potions again in Book 7? I don't think we need to, given how complete this sequence of payoffs has been. But I just wanted to point out the beauty of it all.

And now, with the dramatic concept of set-ups and payoffs fully illustrated and completely clear, let's start looking at the set-ups that *will* be paid off in Book 7.

CHAPTER 3

LORD VOLDEMORT

In looking at set-ups and payoffs throughout *Harry Potter*, we must start with the character who drives the action of the series (as all good villains do): Tom Marvolo Riddle, the Dark Lord, He-Who-Must-Not-Be-Named, Lord Voldemort himself.

What does Lord Voldemort want? And how will he get it?

A lot of people have commented that in *Half-Blood Prince*, we really didn't know what Voldemort was up to. He never even made an appearance. But I think we have enough clues to figure out how he's been keeping himself busy. After all, Voldemort himself has made his overarching goal very clear:

> *"I, who have gone further than anybody along the path that leads to immortality. You know my goal -- to conquer death."* [GF-33]

We've known since *Chamber of Secrets* that part of his goal of conquering death involves killing Harry. We learn more about this goal in each book, culminating in the news of the half-heard prophecy in *Order of the Phoenix*.

Taking the goal of immortality to an extreme, we learned in *Half-Blood Price* about Voldemort's use of Horcruxes. So his primary goal seems pretty straightforward: to foil death.

VOLDEMORT'S POWERS

Let's look at the set-ups and knowledge we already have regarding the powers Voldemort has available in his pursuit of this goal. Doing so will give us a very good sense of what he's been up to in *Half-Blood Prince* and what he might be planning next.

We know Voldemort has dark powers even Dumbledore will never have [SS-1, CS-2]. We know he has *"weapons you can't imagine"* [PA-19]. We know, in Dumbledore's words:

> *"...that Voldemort's knowledge of magic is perhaps more extensive than any wizard alive. I knew that even my most complex and powerful protective spells were unlikely to be invincible if he ever returned to full power."* [OP-37]

We also know the Dark Lord is extremely skilled at Legilimency and Occlumency. Even as an untrained boy who didn't know he was a wizard, Tom Riddle apparently had the ability to make people tell the truth and to know if they were lying [HBP-13]. While at Hogwarts, Slughorn points out that Tom Riddle always seemed to know what he shouldn't know [HBP-17]. Was this from skulking around listening at keyholes? Or from some form of Legilimency?

Related to this, reputedly the Dark Lord can always tell when someone is lying. In Voldemort's own words:

> *"Do not lie to me!"* hissed the second voice. *"I can always tell, Wormtail!"*.... *"Do not lie to Lord Voldemort, Muggle, for he knows... he always knows!"* [GF-1]

(Of course, *we* know Lord Voldemort does *not* always know when someone is lying to him -- because under any interpretation Snape has certainly managed to keep secrets from him.)

What else do we know about Voldemort's abilities that might prove useful in Book 7?

We know Voldemort can leave magical protection behind [HBP-26]. And he has a psychological power that he uses to great effect: The power of fear, with wizards good and evil alike afraid even to say his name. A fear that is still in effect even when the wizarding world has thought him dead for 11 years! We're told right off the bat how to respond to the fear everyone feels:

> *"All this 'You-Know-Who' nonsense -- for eleven years I have been trying to persuade people to call him by his proper name: Voldemort." Professor McGonagall flinched, but Dumbledore, who was unsticking two lemon drops, seemed not to notice. "It all gets so confusing if we keep saying 'You-Know-Who.' I have never seen any reason to be frightened of saying Voldemort's name."* [SS-1]

Outside of what we have seen him do, the above is a pretty exhaustive list of what we know about Voldemort's powers. In other words, not much. But the sheer *fear* with which everyone treats him (and the caution with which Dumbledore treats him) tells us he is powerful indeed.

(Think of the moment we first see Darth Vader in the original *Star Wars* movie. We might be tempted to laugh at the get-up, were it not for two things: the music, and the fact that we see Stormtroopers break out of formation and *run* merely at his appearance on the scene. Other characters' reactions tell us a lot about how *we* are meant to react to a character.)

So back to the main question here: What has Voldemort been up to recently? To answer that, let's take a look at what he *has* done, both when he was in power at the time of Harry's birth, and during year six of our story.

Sirius gives us a good picture of what it's like with Voldemort in control:

> *"Imagine that Voldemort's powerful now. You don't know who his supporters are, you don't know who's working for him and who isn't; you know he can control people so that they do terrible things without being able to stop themselves. You're scared for yourself, and your family, and your friends. Every week, news comes of more deaths, more disappearances, more torturing... the Ministry of Magic's in disarray, they don't know what to do, they're trying to keep everything hidden from the Muggles, but meanwhile, Muggles are dying too. Terror everywhere... panic... confusion... that's how it used to be."* [GF-27]

I think the set-ups are all in place to say that how it "used to be" is how it *is* in the world outside Hogwarts during *Half-Blood Prince*.

Muggles are being killed, sometimes just for fun [GF-9], sometimes as collateral damage when they get in the way of wizard battles [HBP-1]. Wizards are being controlled by the Imperius Curse (as we see with Madam Rosmerta). The Ministry of Magic can't tell anyone what's going on [GF-13]. Families are being torn apart (as the Longbottoms were, as the Boneses are in *Half-Blood Prince*), lives are being ruined [GF-31].

We also know that, in Voldemort's former reign, Aurors were given the power to kill [GF-27]. Is that a set-up that tells us that Harry may have to fight better-trained wizards than himself, wizards who *should* be on the good side, in book 7?

All this gives us a pretty good picture of what life is like in the Wizarding World as of the year of *Half-Blood Prince*. But we have a new weapon to fear going forward...

THE INFERI

What do we know about the Inferi? Let's start with Dumbledore's description:

> *"They are corpses," said Dumbledore calmly. "Dead bodies that have been bewitched to do a Dark wizard's bidding. Inferi have not been seen for a long time, however, not since Voldemort was last powerful.... He killed enough people to make an army of them, of course."* [HBP-4]

We know Inferi are aggressive [HBP-9]. They can be "programmed" to act when the Dark Wizard who bewitched them isn't around. They can "survive" underwater. They can be petrified, they can be stopped by *Impedimenta*, they can be stopped by fire (not coincidentally, the elemental symbol of Gryffindor House) [HBP-26]. And even the wussy Ministry of Magic has had to admit that Inferi may be on the loose once more [HBP-3].

But let's look back at that quote from Dumbledore: He refers to an "army" of Inferi. Now *that's* a scary thought.

It'd be easy to think all the talk of Inferi in *Half-Blood Prince* was just a set-up for Harry and Dumbledore's escape from the Cave at the end of the story. But I don't think so. I think we have been nicely set up for a Book 7 battle against an *army* of Inferi. Infinitely worse than a handful of Death Eaters, maybe even worse than a horde of dementors!

VOLDEMORT AND HOGWARTS

What else will we see from Voldemort in Book 7? Hagrid tells us Voldemort didn't dare try to attack or "take over" Hogwarts while Dumbledore was there [SS-4].

But Dumbledore's not there anymore. And if Voldemort (through his lieutenants) was willing to try a stealth attack on Hogwarts in *Half-Blood Prince* while Dumbledore *was* there, what might he try in Book 7 with Dumbledore gone?

And what *was* that curse about, the one Harry thought he saw Voldemort cast [HBP-20]? Did Voldemort curse *only* the Defense Against the Dark Arts job? There's a question that must be answered in Book 7.

All in all, Voldemort doesn't seem to have finished with Hogwarts yet. The set-ups are certainly there to tell us Voldemort may indeed go back to Hogwarts in Book 7.

VOLDEMORT'S SOUL

One last question about Voldemort for which we have some interesting set-ups is that of the state of his soul. We learn about the importance of the soul in the world of *Harry Potter* when Lupin discusses the Dementor's Kiss:

> *"You can exist without your soul, you know, as long as your brain and heart are still working. But you'll have no sense of self anymore, no memory, no... anything. There's no chance at all of recovery. You'll just -- exist. As an empty shell. And your soul is gone forever... lost."* [PA-12]

Without delving yet into the subject of Horcruxes (that's for a later chapter!), let's think about the state of Voldemort's soul. Two-sevenths of it are already gone with the destruction of the Diary and Ring Horcruxes (maybe three-sevenths, if R.A.B. got another seventh of Voldemort's soul by destroying the Locket Horcrux).

What will this mean for Voldemort? Will he start to lose his memory? His powers? Will he become weaker as the Horcruxes are destroyed?

The answer to this question will make a huge difference to Harry in Book 7. So let's turn to take a look at the main conflict in *Harry Potter*: Harry vs. Voldemort.

CHAPTER 4

VOLDEMORT AND HARRY

When we look at the set-ups concerning the relationship between Voldemort and Harry, much of what we find comes in the "obvious" category, because it's been hammered into our consciousness repeatedly. However, since the Voldemort/Harry relationship is the key to the entire *Harry Potter* story, a review of what we know might not be such a bad idea.

Let's start where the story itself all started:

HARRY'S SCAR

Harry's scar hurts when Voldemort is angry [OP-18]. According to Dumbledore, it hurts when Voldemort is near Harry or feeling a powerful emotion such as hatred [GF-30, OP-37]. We particularly see this played out when Voldemort is angry at the loss of the prophecy [OP-31].

Harry's scar also hurts (no surprise here!) when Voldemort attempts to possess Harry [OP-31]. It hurts when Voldemort, newly returned to his body, presses Wormtail's Dark Mark [GF-33]. In this instance, we see Harry's scar acting as if it were Harry's own version of the Dark Mark, which raises the peripheral question: Does the Dark Mark hurt the Death Eaters? (My guess would be yes. Why wouldn't Voldemort cause pain if he had the opportunity to do so?)

Most interestingly, because it raises the Legilimency/Occlumency question, the scar hurts when Harry looks Dumbledore in the eyes and feels Voldemort's hatred for him [OP-22]:

> But as Dumbledore's fingers closed over Harry's skin, a pain shot through the scar on his forehead, and he felt again that terrible, snake-like longing to strike Dumbledore, to bite him, to hurt him-- [OP-27]

Harry's scar, we know, is the result of the failed Avada Kedavra curse Voldemort shot at Harry [OP-24]. But the real question is: Why did the Avada Kedavra fail? Dumbledore says initially they don't know why it failed [SS-1], and Voldemort certainly doesn't know why:

> "Well," said Riddle, smiling pleasantly, "how is it that you -- a skinny boy with no extraordinary magical talent -- managed to defeat the greatest wizard of all time? How did you escape with nothing but a scar, while Lord Voldemort's powers were destroyed?" [CS-17]

Nevertheless, later Dumbledore explains (though without details) that the Avada Kedavra failed because of Lily's blood sacrifice in dying to save Harry, and that her death provided him with protection [SS-17, CS-17]. (We'll talk more about Lily's sacrifice in Chapter 6.)

The Avada Kedavra gave Harry more than a scar, however. It somehow gave him the powers to escape Voldemort four times (and counting), and it gave him a "destiny" [OP-37].

It also gave him, according to Dumbledore, the tools Harry will need to defeat Voldemort [HBP-23]. Now *there's* a tantalizing set-up! What tools could Harry have that we don't yet know about, that he might draw on in Book 7?

PARSELTONGUE

One of them, perhaps, is the gift of Parseltongue, which doesn't seem to Harry like much of a gift at first. We see (but don't recognize at the time) Parseltongue when Harry sets the boa constrictor free [SS-2], and in the dueling club scene [CS-11]. Two set-ups, which seem to be paid off when Harry uses Parseltongue to reach the Chamber of Secrets [CS-16].

But, as we've noted, J.K. Rowling has a delicious way of *seeming* to pay off a set-up in a small way, but actually holding on to it for an even *bigger* payoff down the line. Is something similar happening with Parseltongue?

We learned in *Half-Blood Prince* that Salazar Slytherin's descendants can speak not just to snakes, but to *each other* in Parseltongue [HBP-10]. Might Harry use Parseltongue to speak directly to Voldemort in Book 7? Perhaps to speak to him in private, though surrounded by, say, Death Eaters -- or members of the Order of the Phoenix -- none of whom would be able to understand them?

Or might Harry use Parseltongue to speak to (and control?) Nagini, one of the Horcruxes he must destroy?... No, I definitely don't think we've seen the end of Parseltongue.

THE HARRY/VOLDEMORT MIND CONNECTION

After Voldemort regains his body, the link between him and Harry grows into something far more than a prickling scar.

Harry now begins to share Voldemort's feelings. He feels Voldemort's jubilation when the Death Eaters break out of Azkaban [OP-24]. He feels Voldemort's anger at Avery while punishing him

[OP-26]. He feels like a snake and wants to attack Dumbledore, echoing Voldemort's hatred of Dumbledore [OP-22]. And he feels Voldemort's burning desire to get the prophecy in a dream (one certainly planted by Voldemort) [OP-23].

More than just feeling, Harry is suddenly able to *see* Voldemort across time and space: He sees the murder of Frank Bryce [GF-1]. He sees Voldemort torture Wormtail [GF-29]. He sees through Voldemort's eyes when Voldemort speaks to Rookwood [OP-26].

In the most notorious moment of this mind-to-mind link, Harry sees through Voldemort's -- and Nagini's -- eyes when Nagini attacks Mr. Weasley in the Ministry of Magic [OP-21]. According to Dumbledore, this moment is the crucial one, the one in which Voldemort detects Harry's presence in his mind [OP-37]. And *that's* a bad thing, because Voldemort can now *manipulate* Harry's mind by planting visions (as in the growing "dreams" where Harry enters the Department of Mysteries).

Voldemort's mental attacks on Harry come to their full fruition when he *plants* the vision of Sirius being tortured [OP-31]. Harry may believe it's true despite Hermione's rightful suspicions, but apparently what Voldemort has been doing is fairly widely known:

> "The little baby woke up fwightened and fort what
> it dweamed was twoo," *said the woman in a horrible, mock-
> baby voice.* [OP-35]

Harry is tortured here and subsequently by his failure to learn Occlumency and keep Voldemort out, by the ease with which Voldemort manipulated him [OP-37]... which brings us to the subject of Occlumency and Legilimency, and their use in the Voldemort/Harry relationship.

OCCLUMENCY AND LEGILIMENCY

Other than Harry's spectacular (and perhaps predictable) failure to learn Occlumency under Snape's tutelage, we are told much too little on this subject.

We do know some fairly obvious facts: We know Harry's ability to detect Voldemort's presence and emotions has become stronger since Voldemort returned to his body [OP-37]. We know Dumbledore, anticipating this, correctly expected Voldemort would try to manipulate Harry's mind in an effort to reach Dumbledore [OP-37]. As Harry tries (so unwillingly) to learn Occlumency, we learn from Snape that Harry's sharing of Voldemort's thoughts and emotions is especially strong while Harry is asleep [OP-24] and that it grows stronger while Harry is learning Occlumency [OP-25].

And that's it! This powerful mind-to-mind connection exists -- a connection so unique that any Death Eater would kill to have it, we're told [HBP-23]. And then it's simply cut off.

All of a sudden, Voldemort slams the mental door shut against Harry at the beginning of *Half-Blood Prince*, and starts employing Occlumency against him [HBP-4]. Supposedly this is because Harry showed in *Order of the Phoenix* that he could enter Voldemort's mind without damage, while Voldemort, in contrast, was unable to possess Harry because of the love in Harry's heart [HBP-23].

But this all seems a bit too easy. Did Harry pose *that* great a danger to Voldemort? Or is this just an easy way to get Voldemort out of the picture during *Half-Blood Prince*? If Harry does pose such a danger, then we definitely should see Harry *try* to employ Legilimency against Voldemort in Book 7.

And by the way, why hasn't Voldemort tried to employ Legilimency against Harry, other than planting images in his brain?

We have no clues laid in whatsoever that Voldemort has tried to learn the Order of the Phoenix's secrets through his link to Harry's mind (other than Dumbledore saying he suspected Voldemort would try to do so).

In fact, the only instance of Voldemort-to-Harry Legilimency we see is when Voldemort can tell that Harry is being truthful about the prophecy being smashed [OP-36].

We have an awful lot of set-up about Legilimency and Occlumency here, and really very little payoff. We must see some mind-to-mind action in some form in Book 7... or we will have to conclude, unfortunately, that Rowling probably shut down the Legilimency/Occlumency connection between Harry and Voldemort because, really, it would make the unraveling of this plotline all too easy.

VOLDEMORT'S AND HARRY'S WANDS

Voldemort and Harry have one more important connection: Their wands.

Voldemort's and Harry's wands share a core: a feather from Fawkes. We learn from Ollivander in the very beginning of the story that this will be significant:

> "...It is very curious indeed that you should be destined for this wand when its brother -- why, its brother gave you that scar.... Curious indeed how these things happen. The wand chooses the wizard, remember.... I think we must expect great things from you, Mr. Potter.... After all, He-Who-Must-Not-Be-Named did great things -- terrible, yes, but great." [SS-5, excerpted]

We see the importance of the relationships between the wands in *Goblet of Fire* when we are introduced to the Priori Incantatem effect:

> *"So what happens when a wand meets its brother?" said Sirius.*
>
> *"They will not work properly against each other," said Dumbledore. "If, however, the owners of the wands force the wands to do battle... a very rare effect will take place. One of the wands will force the other to regurgitate spells it has performed -- in reverse." [GF-36]*

I haven't seen anyone mention the obvious corollary to Dumbledore's statement: The Priori Incantatem effect means Harry and Voldemort cannot fight each other conventionally. Harry cannot count on defeating Voldemort by use of his wand, at least not in a battle.

Now, we sort of knew this already. Dumbledore tells us Harry must defeat Voldemort through love (however vague that pronouncement may seem). And we know Voldemort is a greater wizard (at this point) than Harry, so taking him on wand-to-wand would seem foolhardy.

But after *Goblet of Fire*, the set-up is crystal clear: Any attempt to take on Voldemort magically will not work. We'd better see Harry figure this out and follow through with it in Book 7.

So how *can* Harry destroy Voldemort? We know from the prophecy that *only* Harry can kill Voldemort. Presumably this is why Dumbledore declares in *Half-Blood Prince* that Harry's blood is "more valuable" than his own [HBP-26]. But if Harry can't use his wand, how is this supposed to work?

I think we're given a subtle hint when we see Dumbledore's reaction to the newly-minted Lord Voldemort. Note that Dumbledore insists on continuing to call him "Tom" [HBP-20].

This may be a key to Harry's ability to destroy Voldemort. Perhaps he will have to approach the Dark Lord *not* as Lord Voldemort, but as Tom Riddle. We've seen Harry is indeed capable of feeling a little bit of pity for Tom Riddle (discussed further in Chapter 9). Could this be the secret to the final denouement?

Let's sum up the Voldemort/Harry relationship: Voldemort wants to kill Harry because of his interpretation of the prophecy and because of what happened when his original Avada Kedavra failed. (Note, by the way, that everything Voldemort has done against Harry is based on a lie -- at least on a half-truth -- because he only heard half the prophecy [OP-37]).

On Harry's end, Harry knows he must kill Voldemort. Harry can't kill Voldemort in battle -- but he was given the tools he needs to destroy Voldemort by You-Know-Whom himself, as a consequence of the failed Avada Kedavra. And Dumbledore tells us Harry can only defeat Voldemort through the power of love, as exemplified by Lily's blood sacrifice.

We have some set-ups, but there are some seriously missing pieces here. What tools was Harry given? (Parseltongue? The mind link? Or...?) What does it look like to defeat Voldemort with "love"? What happens if Voldemort learns the entire prophecy?

Perhaps we'll learn more when we go back to Godric's Hollow with Harry. Perhaps the key to the Voldemort/Harry relationship lies in what really happened the night James and Lily were killed.

But for now, we have tantalizingly few set-ups, and fewer payoffs to help us in our speculations.

CHAPTER 5

VOLDEMORT'S FOLLOWERS

THE DEATH EATERS

We actually don't know that much about the Death Eaters -- which isn't all that surprising, since they don't know all that much about each other either [GF-30].

The Death Eaters we know who are still alive include:

Alecto
Amycus
Avery
The Carrows
Crabbe
Goyle (jointly the fathers of... oh you know)
Antonin Dolohov
Fenrir Greyback (a werewolf)
Jugson
Bellatrix, Rodolphus, and Rabastan Lestrange
Macnair (would-be executioner of Buckbeak)
Lucius and Narcissa (Black) Malfoy (Draco's parents)
Mulciber
Nott
Peter Pettigrew (aka Wormtail)
Augustus Rookwood (of the Department of Mysteries)
Travers

Yaxley
The unidentified Big Blond Death Eater

Death Eaters who have died during the books include Karkaroff and Barty Crouch.

Oh, and two other potential Death Eaters: Draco Malfoy. And Severus Snape. (We'll come back to them soon. Each deserves his own chapter -- or more.)

Voldemort's followers were named Death Eaters by the time he returned to Hogwarts to seek employment from Dumbledore, but the name "Death Eaters" was still mostly secret at that time [HBP-20]. The very earliest of Tom Riddle's followers joined him while still at Hogwarts:

> "As he moved up the school, he gathered about him a group of dedicated friends; I call them that, for want of a better term, although as I have already indicated, Riddle undoubtedly felt no affection for any of them. This group had a kind of dark glamour within the castle. They were a motley collection; a mixture of the weak seeking protection, the ambitious seeking some shared glory, and the thuggish gravitating toward a leader who could show them more refined forms of cruelty. In other words, they were the forerunners of the Death Eaters, and indeed some of them became the first Death Eaters after leaving Hogwarts." [HBP-17]

Dumbledore describes these early Death Eaters well: The weak. The ambitious. The thuggish. And today's Death Eaters certainly maintain the characteristics of their forerunners: The weak (Pettigrew). The ambitious (Lucius Malfoy, Bellatrix Lestrange). The thuggish (Macnair).

Dumbledore is, I think, mostly right that Voldemort feels no affection for them. However, I believe this is a result of Voldemort's inability at this point in his transformation to feel *any* affection. Were he able to feel, he probably would care for them. After all, he does call the Death Eaters his "true family" in *Goblet of Fire* [GF-33].

But Voldemort *can't* feel affection for them. So how does he treat them? Not that well, as we might guess.

He is angry with those who are weak. He exploits them, his usage of Quirrell in *Sorcerer's Stone* probably the most blatant instance. He pursues and kills those who leave him (Karkaroff being a prime example, "R.A.B." probably another). His treatment of them is such that Death Eaters who denied him and thereby stayed out of Azkaban after his first downfall are frightened to see him return [GF-9].

We're going to discuss in Chapter 9 Harry's need to summon pity and forgiveness for those who have wronged him. Given that need, it's interesting that Voldemort himself brings up the subject of forgiveness almost as soon as he returns to his body, when he confronts Avery about his disappointment in the Death Eaters who abandoned him:

> *"You ask for forgiveness? I do not forgive. I do not forget. Thirteen long years... I want thirteen years' repayment before I forgive you."* [GF-33]

Voldemort marks his Death Eaters as his own with the Dark Mark, borne on the left forearm. The Mark is also raised supposedly when murder has been committed -- though it's interesting that the only times we've seen the Dark Mark set in the sky, there has been *no* murder: At the Quidditch World Cup in *Goblet of Fire*, and over the Astronomy Tower in *Half-Blood Prince*.

Supposedly only the Death Eaters can conjure the Dark Mark [GF-9] -- but this can't be true, because Dumbledore seems to assume Slughorn *could* have conjured it over the house he was hiding in [HBP-4].

The way Voldemort uses Wormtail's Dark Mark to summon the other Death Eaters raises one small question: Why did Voldemort need to press someone else's Dark Mark? Does Voldemort have a Dark Mark? If not, this is one potential area of vulnerability: Without a Dark Mark himself, he might not be able to summon his followers without another Death Eater at hand. (Of course, he could have other ways to summon them. But none has been set up for us.)

Voldemort cannot be *too* dependent on his followers, however. Yes, they do know his ultimate goal: To be immortal:

> *"And then I ask myself, but how could they have believed I would not rise again? They, who knew the steps I took, long ago, to guard myself against mortal death."* [GF-33]

But apparently Voldemort doesn't trust his Death Eaters all *that* much, as shown by the fact that, when he left the Diary Horcrux with Lucius Malfoy, he didn't tell him the true value of the object. (Had he done so, I have to believe Lucius wouldn't have been so cavalier about palming it off on Ginny).

So given the set-ups we have before us about the Death Eaters, what can we expect in the way of payoffs in Book 7? Well, not much, I have to say.

Looking at the set-up/payoff structure regarding the Death Eaters from a dramatic point of view, I think the Death Eaters are, for the most part, "characters of mass and weight." They're there to add to Voldemort's threat, to give him an army of sorts. (But remember, if we have an army of Inferi coming, there's even less need to keep the Death Eaters in the forefront).

We'll definitely *see* the Death Eaters again, filling out the edges of the screen, as it were, but I don't think many will be of great importance in Book 7. With a couple of individual exceptions, of course: Greyback. Bellatrix. And definitely Wormtail.

THE DEMENTORS

But the Death Eaters aren't Voldemort's only followers. We mustn't forget the Dementors, the Dark Lord's "natural allies" [GF-33].

We've known for some time that the dementors were out of Ministry control. They entered the grounds of Hogwarts when Dumbledore forbade it in *Prisoner of Azkaban*. They allowed the big escape from Azkaban [OP-25]. And, of course, they revolted completely by the end of *Order of the Phoenix* [OP-38].

And they're breeding [HBP-1]. (Yuck. Some mental images are just too gross to imagine.)

I think we will see dementors again in Book 7 -- lots and *lots* of dementors. Who knows, maybe a combined army of dementors and Inferi? (Double yuck.) It's one thing to fight off a single Dementor, or even a group of them, with a single Patronus. But what happens if you're faced with an army of them?

Maybe we'll learn in Book 7 what Snape's alternate method of fighting them is (implied when Harry has to write an essay in *Half-Blood Prince* defending his own method).

In any event, Voldemort will certainly begin Book 7 with ample supporters to keep Harry and the Order of the Phoenix quite busy.

CHAPTER 6

THE DEATHS OF LILY AND JAMES POTTER

WHAT HAPPENED AT GODRIC'S HOLLOW?

The events of the first chapter of the entire *Harry Potter* story are proving to be *the* key events of the entire plot. So let's look at what we know, and what set-ups we might have in front of us yet to be paid off.

We actually know very little about what happened that night. Harry initially only recalls the green flash that we later learn is associated with the Avada Kedavra, plus pain in his forehead [SS-2, SS-6, GF-14]. Later he also hears Voldemort's laugh [SS-4, SS-14]. Through his contact with the dementors, Harry begins to hear Lily and James's voices, and get a fuller (though still sketchy) picture of what happened [PA-9, PA-10, PA-12]:

> *Harry had been picturing his parents' deaths over and over again for three years now, ever since he'd found out they had been murdered, ever since he'd found out what had happened that night: Wormtail had betrayed his parents' whereabouts to Voldemort, who had come to find them at their cottage. How Voldemort had killed Harry's father first. How James Potter had tried to hold him off, while he shouted at his wife to take Harry and run... Voldemort had advanced on Lily Potter, told her to move aside so that he could kill Harry... how she had begged him to kill her instead, refused to stop shielding her son... and so*

Voldemort had murdered her too, before turning his wand on Harry....[GF-14]

It all seems pretty straightforward, except for one thing. Lily didn't have to die. We learn this from a pretty authoritative source, Voldemort himself:

> *"I killed your father first, and he put up a courageous fight... but your mother needn't have died... she was trying to protect you."* [SS-17]

Why? Why didn't Lily have to die? Dumbledore tells us Lily had a choice, presumably to let Voldemort kill Harry and live herself [HB-13]. But Voldemort is not a fountain of mercy. Why would he spare Lily at all?

This is clearly one of the key questions to be answered, and I suspect it will end up wrapped up around the enigmatic Severus Snape. Which raises more questions, especially this one:

HOW WILL HARRY LEARN THE STORY?

Following up on *this* question, we might want to ask: Who else was present at Godric's Hollow when Harry was killed? Did Voldemort go alone? Or was someone else there?

Let's face it, someone had to be there. Voldemort was trashed by the rebounding of the curse. He lost his body. Who carried him away? And who carried his wand away, so that Wormtail could return it to him in *Goblet of Fire*? Was Wormtail there? Or perhaps... Snape?

We do know that Snape learned about the prophecy by listening at the keyhole when Trelawney unwittingly pronounced it to Dumbledore [HBP-25]. However, at least according to Snape, he didn't realize at first that Voldemort would go after the Potters.

Moving a step or two out of the realm of examining set-ups and payoffs and another step across the speculation line: Could Voldemort have been willing to grant Lily's life at the behest of loyal Death Eater Snape?

If so, and if Snape really didn't know ahead of time what Voldemort was about to do, that might mean Snape was on the scene, a potential avenue by which Harry might learn what really happened that night (albeit an unlikely one).

It's not Harry's only potential avenue however. He could learn something from Dumbledore's Pensieve.

What *is* going to happen to Dumbledore's Pensieve in Book 7, anyway? Does it, presumably along with all those little silver instruments, automatically devolve to the next headmaster/mistress of Hogwarts? Or has Dumbledore left a will? (Sirius did, after all.) Could Dumbledore have left the Pensieve to Harry? Or could all Dumbledore's belongings automatically go to his next of kin, presumably Aberforth (whom J.K. Rowling has hinted is a profitable line of inquiry to pursue)?

If Harry *does* get hold of the Pensieve in Book 7, will it give him a full account of what happened? Can an infant's memory "work" in a Pensieve? If it does, we know it will be accurate, as Rowling has assured us in interviews that the Pensieve shows what really happened, not the rememberer's theory of what happened.

I suspect Harry's memory *would* be complete, even though he was an infant. After all, we have the set-up of his memories prompted by the dementors, which include specific dialogue between Lily, James and Voldemort. Remember, the infant Harry would not yet have been able to understand the language being spoken, so the fact that the dementor-induced memories include this dialogue might indicate the possibility of getting fuller memories via the Pensieve.

Given these set-ups, I wouldn't be surprised to see Harry seek out the Pensieve and get the full picture. Who knows --perhaps he will find Snape on the scene (begging for Lily's life?). Or someone else we might recognize...

Other people were certainly on the scene very shortly afterward. Hagrid and Sirius showed up apparently immediately after the murder [PA-10]. How did they know to go there? Harry can't ask Sirius about his parents' death anymore -- but he can ask Hagrid. I think it's time for Harry to (finally!) start asking questions.

And those questions must center on Lily, a character we really first get to hear about in *Half-Blood Prince*. James died, yes. But because Lily died to protect Harry, because she didn't *have* to die, her death is the important one.

LILY'S BLOOD

Somehow the importance of Lily's death is, in an authorial choice wrapped up in profound Christian symbolism, linked to Lily's blood.

Dumbledore laid a charm on 4, Privet Drive that involved Lily's blood and its continuation in Petunia [OP-37]. This blood continues to provide protection for Harry even 16 years later, as both Voldemort and Dumbledore acknowledge:

"For he has been better protected than I think even he knows, protected in ways devised by Dumbledore long ago, when it fell to

him to arrange the boy's future. Dumbledore invoked an ancient magic, to ensure the boy's protection as long as he is in his relations' care. Not even I can touch him there..." [GF-33]

"While you can still call home the place where your mother's blood dwells, there you cannot be touched or harmed by Voldemort. He shed her blood, but it lives on in you and her sister. Her blood became your refuge. You need return there only once a year, but as long as you can still call it home, there he cannot harm you. Your aunt knows this..." [OP-37]

It's interesting, by the way, that Voldemort refers to this use of blood as an "ancient magic," one that he admits he had forgotten [GF-33]. It brings to mind the "Deep Magic" and "Deeper Magic" from C.S. Lewis's *The Lion, The Witch, and the Wardrobe* -- a magic which, in direct allegory to the death of Christ on the cross, also relied on the shedding of blood.

THE 'GLEAM OF TRIUMPH'

We see the importance of blood again when Voldemort returns to his body. He originally couldn't touch Harry in *Sorcerer's Stone*, but after taking in Harry's blood [GF-33], Voldemort is able to touch him without any consequences.

This would seem like a triumph for Voldemort and a step toward defeat for Harry. But apparently there is still something we don't understand about it:

"He said my blood would make him stronger than if he'd used someone else's," Harry told Dumbledore. "He said the protection my -- my mother left in me -- he'd have it too. And he was right -- he could touch me without hurting himself, he touched my face."

For a fleeting instant, Harry thought he saw a gleam of something like triumph in Dumbledore's eyes. But next second, Harry was sure he had imagined it... [GF-36]

What the heck is the Gleam of Triumph, anyway? This is one of *the* questions that Rowling must answer in Book 7. I think she will have cheated us if she doesn't answer it!

So clearly blood -- Lily's blood, Harry's blood -- will continue to be important in Book 7.

Note that we didn't drop the subject of blood in *Half-Blood Prince.* Even though we learned nothing new about Lily's sacrifice, Harry's blood comes up when he and Dumbledore attempt to enter the Cave. When blood is required for entrance, Dumbledore volunteers his own, saying that Harry's is "more valuable [HBP-26]."

Why is Harry's blood more valuable? Clearly, if we put together all the set-ups we've been handed already, it's because his blood holds a key to Voldemort's downfall.

While we're on the subject of Lily's blood, let's detour a second to talk about another link Harry has to Lily:

LILY'S EYES

Harry has Lily's eyes. We learned this immediately -- it's the first thing Hagrid says when he meets Harry:

> *"An' here's Harry!" said the giant.... "Las' time I saw you, you was only a baby," said the giant. "Yeh look a lot like yer dad, but yeh've got yer mom's eyes."* [SS-4]

Hagrid's not the only one. Ollivander says it when he first meets Harry [SS-5], Doge says it [PA-3], even Dumbledore mentions it [PA-27]. Harry himself notices how he has his mother's eyes when he sees Lily in the mirror of Erised [SS-12].

We get a small payoff for Harry having his mother's eyes in *Half-Blood Prince*, when Slughorn is persuaded to come to Hogwarts in the first place because Harry's eyes remind him of Lily's [HBP-4]. A second payoff comes when looking into Harry's eyes persuades Slughorn to give Harry the accurate memory about his Horcrux conversation with Tom Riddle [HBP-22].

These are pretty good payoffs. But given how often Harry having his mother's eyes has been drummed home to us, and given the clever way Rowling has of *seeming* to pay off a set-up, only to lull us into not expecting a bigger payoff later on, I wouldn't be a bit surprised to see this come up again in Book 7. The real question is: Who will be affected by seeing Lily's eyes this time?

We do know one thing about all this backstory: Harry is *finally(!)* going to start looking into it. He is heading for Godric's Hollow near the beginning of Book 7 [HBP-30]. Will being on the scene cause him to remember something? Or will it set him on a journey of trying to find out what really happened? (Via Pensieve? Via talking to his parents' friends? Via talking to Hagrid? Or Snape?)

We have a lot of set-ups here. The payoffs, since we haven't seen them yet, must be coming in Book 7.

CHAPTER 7

HARRY'S OTHER FAMILY

Harry lost his parents in Chapter 1 of *Sorcerer's Stone*. But the rest of the books are filled with other family relationships ripe with dramatic set-ups.

Harry's greatest need may be "love" in his task of defeating Voldemort. However, his greatest need as a character -- and certainly his greatest desire -- is the need for a family. This is spelled out for us in *Sorcerer's Stone* when he looks in the Mirror of Erised and sees not only his parents, but his ancestors [SS-12] -- truly his "heart's desire."

But Harry is not self-pitying about the loss of his family. He actually thinks Neville, with his parents alive but tortured to insanity and unable to recognize or speak to their son, has it much worse than he does [GF-31]. This lack of self-pity on Harry's part is, I believe, one of the prime reasons we care for him so much.

And let's face it, if he *wanted* to feel sorry for himself, he sure would have good cause to, given the family he's stuck with:

THE DURSLEYS

As soon as Harry learns he might have other options, he

understandably doesn't want to live with the Dursleys. He certainly doesn't want to return to Privet Drive every summer [PA-3], where he feels cut off from the magical world.

However, despite the Dursleys' denial of the wizarding world, Petunia knows more about it than we would have initially believed. When Dudley is attacked by dementors, Petunia knows what this means [OP-2]. More than that, she knows enough to be deathly afraid of Lord Voldemort:

> *...And all of a sudden, for the very first time in his life, Harry fully appreciated that Aunt Petunia was his mother's sister. He could not have said why this hit him so very powerfully at this moment. All he knew was that he was not the only person in the room who had an inkling of what Lord Voldemort being back might mean. Aunt Petunia had never in her life looked at him like that before. Her large, pale eyes (so unlike her sister's) were not narrowed in dislike or anger: They were wide and fearful.* [OP-2]

(By the way, note yet another reference to Lily's eyes.)

This raises the question: Why has Harry never asked Petunia about his mother? Sure, as a young boy, mistreated as he was, he may never have felt the need to, or he may have felt intimidated. But I would think that, as he returns to Privet Drive in Book 7, knowing it will be his last time there, he should be quizzing Petunia up one side and down the other. What does she know about Lily? What does she know about James? And what *was* in that letter from Dumbledore [SS-1]?

Harry does know about the letter: He heard Hagrid tell the Dursleys about it [SS-4]. And though he doesn't make the connection to it when Dumbledore sends the Howler in *Order of the Phoenix* [OP-2], eventually Dumbledore tells him about it [OP-37].

We know at least a little about what the letter included. It describes the protection over Harry that exists at Privet Drive:

> *"While you can still call home the place where your mother's blood dwells, there you cannot be touched or harmed by Voldemort. He shed her blood, but it lives on in you and her sister. Her blood became your refuge. You need return there only once a year, but as long as you can still call it home, there he cannot hurt you. Your aunt knows this. I explained what I had done in the letter I left, with you, on her doorstep. She knows that allowing you houseroom may well have kept you alive for the past fifteen years."*   [OP-37]

But does the letter say anything else about James's and Lily's death? Does Petunia still have it? If she does (and, compulsive as she is, I expect she would keep it), it sure would seem to be time for Harry to *start asking questions!*

Another important question to be paid off in Book 7 about the Dursleys: We learn in *Half-Blood Prince* that the protection afforded to Harry at Privet Drive will cease the moment Harry turns 17 [HBP-3]. Harry in fact will return to Privet Drive one more time just to take advantage of that protection, per Dumbledore's request of him [HBP-30].

But what happens then? Voldemort certainly knows a good deal about the "ancient magic" protecting Harry. Does he know about this provision? Will he be waiting for Harry's birthday (the date of which he also knows)? What happens to the Dursleys if Voldemort shows up at Privet Drive just as the protection is removed? Will Harry have to fight to save the Dursleys? (Or will he celebrate his birthday at, say, the Weasleys', on his way to Bill and Fleur's wedding, thus avoiding the whole possibility of an attack on the Dursleys?)

The Dursleys aren't the only "family" Harry has, of course. He oh so briefly enjoyed a real live parent figure (of sorts!) in his godfather...

SIRIUS BLACK

For all too short a time, Sirius indeed served as family emotionally for Harry. Not only is Harry ecstatic about even the possibility of living with Sirius [GF-2], but when he truly needs a parent, Sirius is the one he turns to:

> *What he really wanted (and it felt almost shameful to admit it to himself) was someone like -- someone like a parent:, an adult wizard whose advice he could ask without feeling stupid, someone who cared about him, who had had experience with Dark Magic....*
>
> *And then the solution came to him. It was so simple, and so obvious, that he couldn't believe it had taken so long -- Sirius.* [GF-2]

Dumbledore acknowledges the importance of Sirius to Harry *as* family, when he compares Sirius's death to the loss of Harry's family -- a comparison Dumbledore, I feel sure, would not have made lightly [OP-37].

But Sirius is dead now. So whom does Harry have left?

Well, they may not be family by blood or by religious ceremony and commitment... but Harry still has a family:

THE WEASLEYS

Harry likes being treated as family by the Weasleys. We can tell when we see how pleased he is at getting a hug and kiss from Molly [PA-5].

Molly especially treats Harry as her own son in many ways. She and Bill come to see Harry in the third task in the Triwizard Tournament [GF-31]. After the tournament, Molly comforts him as a mother would comfort a son:

> *He could feel a burning, prickling feeling in the inner corners of his eyes. He blinked and stared up at the ceiling.*
>
> *"It wasn't your fault, Harry," Mrs. Weasley whispered.*
>
> *"I told him to take the cup with me," said Harry.*
>
> *Now the burning feeling was in his throat too. He wished Ron would look away.*
>
> *Mrs. Weasley set the potion down on the bedside cabinet, bent down, and put her arms around Harry. He had no memory of ever being hugged like this, as though by a mother. The full weight of everything he had seen that night seemed to fall in upon him as Mrs. Weasley held him to her...* [GF-36]

We see over and over again how Mrs. Weasley cares for Harry as a son -- and not just in the jumpers she knits for him every Christmas! When she sees her family dead while trying to get rid of the Boggart at 12, Grimmauld Place, she sees Harry dead right along with her own children [OP-9]. When Harry starts to back off at St. Mungo's so just the Weasley family can go in and see the injured Mr. Weasley, Molly pulls him in as one of the family [OP-

22]. She also verbalizes her acceptance of Harry as a son, even while Sirius is still alive:

> "...*speaking as someone who has got Harry's best interests at heart--*"
>
> "*He's not your son,*" *said Sirius quietly.*
>
> "*He's as good as,*" *said Mrs. Weasley fiercely.* "*Who else has he got?*" [OP-5]

Frankly, it's these deep emotional links to the Weasleys that made me feel as far back as *Chamber of Secrets* that Harry and Ginny were destined to be together. It's nice for Harry to have a girlfriend, of course, but he doesn't *need* a girlfriend. He *needs* a family. In hooking up with Ginny (assuming things continue on to marriage), Harry gets the family that he needs.

This is not to say, of course, that Harry would ever forget his own family. Much as he appreciates Mrs. Weasley, she can never fully take the place of Lily:

> *Would Neville's mother have died to save him, as Lily had died for Harry? Surely she would.... But what if she had been unable to stand between her son and Voldemort? Would there then have been no "Chosen One" at all? An empty seat where Neville now sat and a scarless Harry who would have been kissed good-bye by his own mother, not Ron's?* [HP-7]

As we wrap up this subject, it's important to note that Harry is not the only one feeling the lack of a family. We learn in *Half-Blood Prince* that Tom Riddle was obsessed with learning about his parentage while at Hogwarts [HBP-17]. Dumbledore and Harry's journeys through the Pensieve take us through Tom Riddle's search and disappointment. We also learn that Hogwarts served to fill the emotional gap, at least to a certain extent, for Tom, who (like Harry, it is important to note) never felt truly at home anywhere but at Hogwarts [HBP-20].

And we see that Voldemort, even in his emotional sterility and evilness, felt the need to, in essence, *manufacture* a "family" -- and to think of them in those terms -- in the Death Eaters:

"... But look, Harry! My true family returns...."

The air was suddenly full of the swishing of cloaks. Between graves, behind the yew tree, in every shadowy space, wizards were Apparating... [GF-33]

Somehow I think Book 7 will hold a happier ending for Harry's search for his family than for Voldemort's pitiful attempts to manufacture one.

CHAPTER 8

LIFE-DEBTS

"...You did a very noble thing, in saving Pettigrew's life."

"But if he helps Voldemort back to power--!"

"Pettigrew owes his life to you. You have sent Voldemort a deputy who is in your debt.... When one wizard saves another wizard's life, it creates a certain bond between them... and I'm much mistaken if Voldemort wants his servant in the debt of Harry Potter."

"I don't want a connection with Pettigrew!" said Harry. "He betrayed my parents!"

"This is magic at its deepest, its most impenetrable, Harry. But trust me... the time may come when you will be very glad you saved Pettigrew's life." [PA-22]

We've gone three books with no sign of this prediction of Dumbledore's coming true. Sure, we've seen Pettigrew again. We've seen him grovel to Voldemort in *Goblet of Fire*, we've seen him grovel to Snape in *Half-Blood Prince*. And most notably, we've seen him help Voldemort regain his own body in *Goblet of Fire*.

But we certainly haven't seen any moment when Harry could conceivably be "glad [he] saved Pettigrew's life."

Yet J.K. Rowling has promised us such a moment is coming. In her 7/16/05 interview posted on The Leaky Cauldron, in response to a question regarding whether Ginny owes a life-debt to Harry dating back to *Chamber of Secrets*, Rowling responds, "No, not really. Wormtail is different. You know, part of me would just love to explain the whole thing to you, plot of book seven, you know, I honestly would."

Practically a promise that Peter Pettigrew will be crucial in Book 7.

WHO MIGHT HAVE A LIFE-DEBT TO HARRY?

Harry has been responsible for saving quite a few lives, enough to justify Hermione's comments about his "saving the world" complex. Before we dive into the subject of Peter in greater depth, let's take a quick look at the people who might owe life-debts of some kind to Harry.

Harry saved Sirius from the dementors in *Prisoner of Azkaban* [PA-20]. Sirius repaid that life-debt in the Battle at the Ministry of Magic where he fought for, and then died for, Harry [OP-35].

Harry saved Arthur Weasley (indirectly) from Nagini [OP-21]; even if that event is subject to some interpretation, Molly gives Harry credit for doing so [OP-22]. So will Arthur have to die for Harry? Given J.K. Rowling's penchant for killing off Harry's father figures (James, Sirius, Dumbledore), and given her recent statement that two people will die in Book 7 whom she didn't originally intend to die (Arthur and Molly?), the set-ups are certainly there. While we all certainly don't want to see Arthur die, if he must, wouldn't we rather see him go down defending Harry (and repaying that debt) than sitting in a hallway somewhere?

Harry has saved the life of more than one Weasley. He saved Ginny in *Chamber of Secrets*, but the Rowling interview mentioned just above specifically states that particular incident didn't create a life-debt between them.

Harry has also saved Ron's life by being so handy with a bezoar when Ron drank the poisoned mead [HBP-18]. Does this create a life-debt between Ron and Harry? Presumably yes, and one which Ron has already stated he's willing to repay. (Notice that though Hermione includes herself in the promise being made, it's Ron who voices it.)

"We'll be there, Harry," said Ron.

"What?"

"At your aunt and uncle's house," said Ron. "And then we'll go with you wherever you're going." [HBP-30]

I do not believe Ron and Hermione will die in Book 7 -- primarily because I believe Rowling, taking death as seriously as she does, would not put her young readers through such a violation. But could there be other ways of repaying a debt?

With Harry having saved the lives of so many Weasleys, perhaps the best way they could repay him would be to take him into their family (by marriage or some less formal means), in essence giving him a life, a future, a hope.

(Harry has, of course, also saved the life of his cousin Dudley [HBP-1]. However, Dumbledore's words regarding the life-debt are quite specific: The situation involves a *wizard* saving another *wizard's* life. So I think no life-debt applies between Harry and Dudley.)

Yes, Harry has saved quite a few lives for a 16-year-old boy.

But none is more important than his saving of Peter Pettigrew.

PETER PETTIGREW

Harry had every reason to let Sirius and Lupin kill Pettigrew [PA-19]. He had just learned Pettigrew was responsible for the deaths of his parents, and revenge for *that* wrongdoing would be sweet indeed. Instead, Harry chooses to show mercy.

Harry's need to show pity to those who have harmed him is going to be significant in book 7. We've already seen pointed set-ups showing Harry feeling pity for Snape, Draco, and Tom Riddle, and Dumbledore has made a point of commenting on these moments. One of the reasons Harry's saving Pettigrew's life is so crucial is, I believe, because it's the first time he shows significant pity toward someone who doesn't deserve it -- a situation I suspect Harry will come up against in Book 7. (More on the importance of pity and forgiveness in Harry's life in the next chapter.)

I see several parallels between Harry's sparing Peter's life and other life-or-death moments in the books. Harry places himself between Pettigrew and the wands of Sirius and Lupin, just as Lily placed herself between Harry and Voldemort's wand. And we can be certain Harry would have placed his body between Dumbledore and Draco's wand, had he been able to do so.

(Instead, note that *Draco* takes Harry's place, as it were, forced into the same psychological and spiritual moment of maturation that Harry went through with Wormtail. Draco's lowering of his wand indicates, I think, the possibility in his soul for forgiveness -- though he is stopped in the process by the Death Eaters.)

With Pettigrew owing an unsettled life-debt to Harry, we are guaranteed to see him again in book 7. Why would we even have been reminded of his presence in *Half-Blood Prince*, really a throwaway moment, if we weren't going to see him again? So the real question is: Will the little rat save Harry's life?

It's hard to imagine, but it could happen. Certainly Pettigrew is a link to the two people Harry will definitely want to find in Book 7: Voldemort and Snape. Is that enough to satisfy a life-debt? Probably not. But somehow Pettigrew's life-debt to Harry will be satisfied in book 7. And Harry will be glad he saved Peter's life.

WHOM MIGHT HARRY OWE A LIFE-DEBT TO?

Life-debts work both ways. And while Harry has saved quite a few lives, he's been on the receiving end of lifesaving as well.

First and foremost, Lily Potter saved her infant son's life by a powerful act of sacrificial love. Yes, James was also killed saving Harry, but Lily "didn't have to die." She *chose* to sacrifice herself for her son. Had she not done so, *Harry Potter* wouldn't even exist.

Harry has been increasingly aware, as he grows in his knowledge of what happened that night, that he must pay that debt by killing the person who killed his mother. He takes a step forward in this understanding in what we might think of as the free will/predestination discussion in the "Horcruxes" chapter of *Half-Blood Prince*:

> "But sir," said Harry, making valiant efforts not to sound argumentative, "it all comes to the same thing, doesn't it? I've got to try and kill him, or--"
>
> "Got to?" said Dumbledore. "Of course you've got to! But not because of the prophecy! Because you, yourself, will never rest until you've tried! We both know it! Imagine, please, just for a moment, that you had never heard that prophecy! How would you

feel about Voldemort now? Think!"

Harry watched Dumbledore striding up and down in front of him, and thought. He thought of his mother, his father, and Sirius. He thought of Cedric Diggory. He thought of all the terrible deeds he knew Lord Voldemort had done. A flame seemed to leap inside his chest, searing his throat.

"I'd want him finished," said Harry quietly. "And I'd want to do it." [HBP-23]

This is one life-debt that must be paid in Book 7. Harry will understand more of what happened the night of his parents' death when he actually visits Godric's Hollow. Then the boy with "his mother's eyes" will go onward to avenge the life-debt he owes to her.

(Interesting to note, however, that Dumbledore says Harry will never rest until he's "tried" -- not until he's actually killed Voldemort. Hmmm.)

Harry also owes a life-debt, presumably, to Dumbledore -- and by extension Fawkes -- who saved Harry in the Battle at the Ministry of Magic [OP-37]. Harry tried to repay the life-debt by saving Dumbledore in the Cave [HBP-26].

This is the moment where the torch passes figuratively from Dumbledore to Harry, as made clear through the much-noted parallel comments by Dumbledore at the beginning and end of *Half-Blood Prince*:

"...I do not think you need worry about being attacked tonight."

"Why not, sir?"

"You are with me," said Dumbledore simply.   [HBP-4]

Paralleled near the end of the book by:

> *"It's going to be all right, sir," Harry said over and over again.... "Don't worry."*

> *"I am not worried, Harry," said Dumbledore, his voice a little stronger despite the freezing water. "I am with you."* [HBP-26]

But Dumbledore is dead. Harry didn't succeed in saving his life. So does Harry still owe him a life-debt?

If he does, he can now repay it by finishing Dumbledore's quest to bring down Voldemort. Which raises the interesting question: Given the events at the end of *Half-Blood Prince,* will Harry get sidetracked from the real quest by his need to avenge Dumbledore by killing Snape? This is probably the largest temptation looming before Harry in Book 7.

Which brings us to the last person who has saved Harry's life: Severus Snape.

As a foreshadowing all the way back in *Sorcerer's Stone,* Snape saved Harry when Quirrell tried to hex him at the Quidditch game [SS-11].   This set-up is paid off later (though Harry certainly wouldn't acknowledge it!) when Snape keeps the other Death Eaters from performing the Cruciatus Curse on Harry [HBP-28]. Snape also doesn't deliver Harry into Voldemort's hands when he has every opportunity to do so (and when his avowed loyalty to the Dark Lord would presumably demand it).

So does Harry now owe a life-debt to Snape? What an interesting dilemma to put Harry in. I'm sure Harry doesn't mind being in debt to his mother or to Dumbledore, just as Arthur and Ron don't mind being in debt to Harry. But Harry may mind *very* much owing a life-debt to Snape (much as Peter Pettigrew must resent owing Harry his life)!

How will Harry repay his life-debt to Snape? He certainly won't die for him -- in fact, I think it much more likely, as several people have suggested, that Snape ends up playing the Sidney Carton role from *A Tale of Two Cities* and goes to *his* death for Harry.

Could Harry pay his debt by taking Dumbledore's place (as he is already starting to do in other ways) as the one person who trusts Snape? Or by willingly putting his life into Snape's hands? By forgiving Snape for his role in the death of his parents? By learning to, in some way, love Snape as Dumbledore evidently managed to do?

The Snape-Harry relationship is shaping up to be *the* key relationship in this entire story. Seeing their relationship through the prism of recognizing the existence of a life-debt between them, which creates a powerful "bond"... well, it certainly lets us know what to watch for in Book 7!

There's one more life-debt to keep in mind: Snape's debt to James for saving his life [SS-17]. What does it mean that Snape owes his life to Harry's father, a man he hated desperately, a man in whose death he may have been complicit [HBP-25]? ...More on Snape's life-debt, and what it means to his relationship to Harry in Chapter 21.

CHAPTER 9

WHAT DOES HARRY NEED TO DO NEXT?

Yes, yes, yes, we all know Harry needs to find the four remaining Horcruxes, destroy them, then kill Lord Voldemort. Ho-hum. Is that all?

We'll come back to the subject of Horcruxes. But first let's look at the set-ups and payoffs around the edges of Harry's Big Task. I want to look first at the people Harry needs to contact to be equipped to take on the task. And I want to look at Harry's *inner* task: The need to forgive.

First, let's look at the people Harry might want to track down:

HIS PARENTS' FRIENDS

Many people have commented on how very incurious Harry is about the past. There are plenty of people around who knew his parents, yet somehow Sirius and Lupin are the only ones he ever talks to about them.

In *Sorcerer's Stone*, Hagrid very kindly sent away to lots of Harry's friends for pictures of James and Lily and made a little scrapbook for him [SS-16]. Well, not only have we never seen that scrapbook again, but Harry has never talked either to Hagrid or to any of the folks in that picture about James and Lily.

We get another photograph into the past when Moody shows Harry a picture of the original Order of the Phoenix [OP-9]. And this time we get names. Sure, most of them are dead, but there are still plenty of people alive who knew the Potters, and several who knew them well. Not only is Lupin still alive, but so are Dedalus Diggle, Hagrid, Elphias Doge, Aberforth Dumbledore, and of course, Mad-Eye Moody himself. (Not to mention other members of the order not in the photo, such as the Weasleys, Professor McGonagall and Severus Snape.)

Since so much in Book 7 would seem to hinge on what happened at Godric's Hollow, and since we have so many people alive who were around at the time and involved with James and Lily, wouldn't it be a good idea for Harry to chat with one or two? Just a thought. Hmmm. Wonder who he should start with...

Wait. Let's look back at that list again. How about...

ABERFORTH DUMBLEDORE

Aberforth, as we know, is Albus Dumbledore's rather strange brother. Apparently quite the animal-lover, we learn from Dumbledore that Aberforth was once prosecuted for practicing inappropriate charms on a goat [GF-24]. Goats come up again when Harry first visits the Hog's Head pub in Hogsmeade:

> *The Hog's Head bar comprised one small, dingy, and very dirty room that smelled strongly of something that might have been goats.* [OP-16]

Harry also pays special attention to the barman:

> *The barman sidled toward them out of a back room. He was a grumpy-looking old man with a great deal of long gray*

hair and beard. He was tall and thin and looked vaguely familiar to Harry. [OP-16]

That combination of set-ups has led some fans to surmise that Aberforth is, in fact, the barman at the Hog's Head -- and J.K. Rowling confirmed this in a 2004 interview.

Q: *"Why is the barman of the Hog's Head vaguely familiar to Harry? Is he Dumbledore's brother?"*

JKR: *"Ooh-- you are getting good. Why do you think that it is Aberforth? [Audience member: Various clues. He smells of goats and he looks a bit like Dumbledore]. I was quite proud of that clue. That is all that I am going to say. [Laughter]. Well, yes, obviously. I like the goat clue -- I sniggered to myself about that one."*

What else do we know about Aberforth? Well, we know he had some sort of dealings with Mundungus (for good or not, we don't know) while Mundungus was purloining and selling off Sirius's stuff [HBP-12]. We know he and Dumbledore were friends [HBP-20] and that he attended Dumbledore's funeral [HBP-30]. And his most important role (that we know of) in the story so far: He is the person who stopped Snape from overhearing the entire prophecy about Voldemort and Harry [HBP-25].

But he may have more of a role to play. While I do really want to look just at set-ups and payoffs *within* the books, not relying on what Rowling may have said, her interviews are pretty much the main source of information on this topic. In her publication-day interview during the summer of 2006 she said:

"Dumbledore's family would be a profitable line of inquiry..."

Well, the only family we know of is Aberforth. If there's other family Harry should know about, Aberforth is clearly the link to get to them. So let's see Harry make the connection about the goats, and head to the Hog's Head to ask some questions about Professor Dumbledore.

There's one other person whom Harry might track down in Book 7, though it may be a bit tougher because he's dead:

R.A.B.

Rowling has come so close to confirming that "R.A.B." is Regulus Black (in fact, the confirmation was temporarily posted online on the Harry Potter Lexicon) that I am going to assume they are one and the same.

Regulus was a Slytherin, one of Slughorn's students [HBP-4]. He became a Death Eater, but backed out. Sirius believed Regulus wasn't important enough to have been killed by Voldemort personally [OP-6]. But what if Sirius was wrong?

We learn from Lupin that Regulus only stayed alive a few days after deserting Voldemort [HBP-6]. That jibes nicely with Dumbledore's statements in the Cave that Voldemort would not want the green potion to kill anyone who drank it *immediately*, because he would want to keep anyone clever enough to *get* to the potion alive for questioning [HBP-26].

So what if Regulus defied Voldemort, located the Locket Horcrux, took it, and left a note:

To the Dark Lord

I know I will be dead long before you read this but I want you to know that it was I who discovered your secret. I have stolen the real Horcrux and intend to destroy it as soon as I can. I face death in the hope that when you meet your match, you will be mortal once more.

R.A.B. [HBP-28]

What if, at that point, R.A.B. either was killed by Voldemort, or died from drinking the potion? I think this the most likely scenario -- and a huge clue that will lead Harry to the location of the *real* Locket Horcrux. Harry, Ron and Hermione haven't figured it out yet, of course, but they're trying [HBP-29, 30]. I doubt it will be long before Hermione puts "R" and "B" together and comes up with the right answer.

But finding the folks that can set him on the right track -- even finding the Horcruxes themselves -- is not all Harry has to accomplish in Book 7.

In Chapter 3, we realized Harry can't defeat Voldemort in direct battle. In any event, Voldemort is a *far* more powerful wizard than Harry -- Dumbledore even acknowledges, as we've seen, that Voldemort was more powerful than *he* was in some ways.

So Harry must defeat Voldemort -- somehow -- by the most powerful force in the universe: Love.

What does this look like? I haven't got a clue, frankly. And I'm glad. I'd really *like* to be surprised in this particular battle.

But we do have some set-ups to partially illumine the way for us. And they come in the areas of...

PITY AND FORGIVENESS

Yes, forgiveness from the young man who keeps trying to cast one of the *Unforgivable* Curses. (Clearly the concept of forgiveness is rooted deep in the wizarding world's consciousness.)

Harry has a lot of people to forgive. There's Draco, for treating him so badly. Snape, for his role in killing James and Lily (not to mention six years of horrible treatment). And -- the biggie -- Voldemort, for killing his parents.

Can Harry forgive them? It's a good question.

We know Harry *can* feel pity, and feel it for those for whom others have nothing but contempt. He feels pity for the unlovable Filch when Mrs. Norris is petrified [CS-9]. He feels pity for the odd Luna Lovegood when all her stuff is stolen [OP-38].

And he takes a huge step toward one of his hardest tasks in Book 7 when he feels pity for Draco Malfoy after Dumbledore's death:

> *Harry did not believe that Malfoy would have killed Dumbledore. He despised Malfoy still for his infatuation with the Dark Arts, but now the tiniest drop of pity mingled with his dislike. Where, Harry wondered, was Malfoy now, and what was Voldemort making him do under threat of killing him and his parents?* [HBP-30]

Note that Harry is, for the first time, relating to Draco in terms he, Harry, understands most intimately: The loss of a family at Voldemort's hands. I think Harry is well on the way to bridging the formerly insurmountable gap between himself and Draco.

As for forgiving Voldemort, which would seem the most

difficult task of all -- Well, Harry has already made some steps in that direction, too. He feels pity (which Dumbledore notes most pointedly) for Tom Riddle when Tom's mother dies [HBP-13]. He understands how Tom felt about Hogwarts [HBP-21], and feels pity for him having to go back to the orphanage if Hogwarts had to close [CS-15].

I think this is the secret to Harry's eventual forgiveness of Voldemort (or however close he can get to actual forgiveness): He must relate to him as Tom Riddle. He must relate to him, in fact, as Dumbledore has done throughout the books, even refusing to use Voldemort's assumed name.

Much has been made of the likeness between Tom Riddle and Harry. Well, if to understand all truly *is* to forgive all, Harry certainly understands much of Tom's background... and this understanding may lead (somehow) to Tom's eventual downfall.

But, as of the end of *Half-Blood Prince*, Harry now has a harder task even than forgiving Voldemort: Forgiving Severus Snape.

For a while, it looked as if there might be some connection between Harry and Snape, albeit a thin one. Harry certainly feels understanding for the young Snape after trespassing on "Snape's Worst Memory" [OP-28, 29]. In discussing the incident with Sirius and Lupin, he almost takes Snape's side [OP-29]. And his appreciation of the Half-Blood Prince [HBP-12, 15, 16] could have led to a real appreciation of Snape in person -- had not Snape killed (or appeared to kill?) Dumbledore, putting him seemingly forever beyond the reach of Harry's forgiveness [HBP-30].

We were set up for Harry's refusal to forgive Snape when Harry refused to feel pity for Kreacher after Sirius's death [OP-37]. And, true to form, Harry consciously and deliberately decides -- more than once, even -- that he will *not* forgive Snape, first after

Sirius's death:

> *...at the sight of [Snape] Harry felt a great rush of hatred beyond anything he felt toward Malfoy.... Whatever Dumbledore said, he would never forgive Snape... never...* [OP-38]

And again after Dumbledore's death:

> *He had loathed Snape from their first encounter, but Snape had placed himself forever and irrevocably beyond the possibility of Harry's forgiveness by his attitude toward Sirius.* [HBP-8]

"Forever and irrevocably." That sounds pretty firm. Yet how can Harry defeat Voldemort by love with all this hatred of Snape in his heart?

I'm not the first person to bring up the question "How can Harry learn to forgive Snape?" and I've participated in some fascinating discussions on the subject. Most of these discussions have centered around Harry learning that Snape really *is* "Dumbledore's man through and through," and using this concept as a first step toward understanding and forgiveness.

But one day it struck me: What if Harry *doesn't* forgive Snape?

What if, just to spin a scenario, Snape were to die for Harry? What if Snape turns out to be the Sidney Carton character of this series, as proposed in Chapter 8? How might Harry's head (and heart) spin around if Snape were to sacrifice himself for Harry?

I absolutely believe Harry when he vows to himself that he will never forgive Severus Snape. If he indeed cannot forgive Snape, such a scenario might just be inevitable.

CHAPTER 10

MAGICAL CREATURES: THE HOUSE-ELVES

We've spent a lot of time looking at the set-ups and payoffs involving our major characters, Voldemort and Harry. Let's take a little detour now and talk about some of the non-human characters that populate *Harry Potter*, the House-Elves.

I think we Muggles tend to think of House-Elves as rather humorous characters. And no wonder, given that we met Dobby as our first example. But House-Elves actually have an astonishing amount of magical power.

First, House-Elves are able to do the seeming impossible: They can Apparate and Disapparate around Hogwarts. This is explained as being necessary for them to do their duties. Okay, fine.

But they also can Apparate *into* Hogwarts (as Kreacher does when Harry sends him there in *Half-Blood Prince* [HBP-3]) and *out of* Hogwarts (as Dobby does after Harry frees him [CS-18]). If what we've been told about Apparition at Hogwarts is true, this is pretty remarkable.

House-Elves' magic is not limited to Apparition, however. Dobby bewitches a Bludger to chase Harry in *Chamber of Secrets* [CS-10]. House-Elves even have power over wizards: Winky "binds" Barty Crouch at the Quidditch World Cup [GF-35]. Dobby knocks Lucius Malfoy down the stairs the minute he's no longer in Malfoy's service [CS-38]. And all this without a wand.

House-Elves aren't permitted to use wands, in fact [GF-9]. Which raises the question: What if they could? Would use of a wand perhaps magnify their already-considerable powers? Let's put a pin in that intriguing thought and move on to how House-Elves are treated by wizards.

And the answer to that is: Not very well. The very first thing we learn about House-Elves is that they are not treated as equals to wizards [CS-2]. While they were admittedly treated worse when Voldemort was in power [CS-10], and while at least the 100 or so House-Elves at Hogwarts appear to receive decent treatment and to be happy [GF-21], their very identity (and even their species name!) is tied up in the fact of their servitude. And even though they have virtually no independence, they can still be convicted of crimes, with the Ministry of Magic predisposed, as in Hokey's case, to suspect them [HBP-20].

That servitude (Hermione would call it slavery) includes some pretty severe limitations. House-Elves are bound to serve one family forever, unless freed by that family. They are bound so strongly to keep that family's secrets that, even when freed, they find it hard to break that bind [GF-21]. (Although, as we see when Kreacher leaves 12, Grimmauld Place, they can find ways to work around this if they really try [OP-37]).

All of this raises the question: What *could* Dobby say about Lucius Malfoy? Does he have information Harry might need? Or what could Kreacher say about Sirius... or about Regulus? Or about that locket we found when cleaning 12, Grimmauld Place?

And the real question, given how incurious he has tended to be: Will Harry *ask*?

Given the treatment most House-Elves receive, it's perhaps not surprising that Hermione, who doesn't share the taught-from-birth prejudices of the wizarding world, comes up with S.P.E.W., the Society for the Promotion of Elvish Welfare, in response to what she views as gross injustices heaped upon the House-Elves. S.P.E.W., despite Hermione's promotion, never catches on.

But we sure spent a lot of time on it, didn't we? Why, we should ask. Was it just a tangent? Was it just comic relief? Was it a thematic detour, to point us to the continuing issue of prejudice, reflected in the main plot lines as pureblood vs. half-blood vs. "mudblood"?

Given all the set-up time expended on S.P.E.W., I'd sure like to hope (though I wouldn't make a firm prediction on this) that we'd see a further payoff to the situation of the House-Elves in general.

Let me just note that we don't *need* a payoff to the House-Elf storyline. If Harry fails to find, or to look for, all four Horcruxes, book 7 will be seriously deficient. But if we never see another House-Elf, the final story will not be deficient... it will simply mean we spent a *lot* of time on things like S.P.E.W. with no payoff on the storyline. And that would be disappointing.

Let's assume there will be a payoff. What might it look like?

Putting together their absolute obedience to their masters with the power that House-Elves can (but are not allowed to) wield, we should ask: What if the House-Elves took sides in the battle against Voldemort? Given their innate understanding of what it means to be downtrodden, it's almost impossible to imagine most of them choosing Voldemort's side.

So what if they fought for the Order of the Phoenix? Voldemort is raising various armies. It would seem that the Order might have one practically ready-made. An army that's fanatically devoted. An army with the ability to go places other wizards can't. An army who can fight without a wand.

That army, if needed, is ready and waiting. But will anyone think to ask....?

CHAPTER 11

MORE MAGICAL CREATURES: THE GOBLINS

Boy, those goblins are revolting.

We're heard about Goblin rebellions in just about every *Harry Potter* book, beginning in year 1 [SS-13].

The Goblins rebelled in 1612 (a rebellion that included particularly "vicious" riots) using the Hogsmeade Inn as their headquarters [PA-5]. But that was just the beginning. There were multiple Goblin rebellions in the 17th century [GF-15], followed by Goblin riots in the 18th century [OP-31]. We also know the Goblins wanted to attend the first International Confederation of Wizards during that era, but they were ousted [OP-7].

So what's the status of the Goblins now? Well, they may not have been accepted as equals by the wizards, but they sure could control the entire Wizarding World if they wanted to, given that they seem to run the wizarding economy. They run Gringotts [SS-5], and as Ludo Bagman knows all too well, they also run what appears to be a variety of loan-sharking and betting operations [GF-26, 37]. Let's face it, if the Goblins wanted to, they could tie the wizarding world up in one big knot.

Our next question therefore must be: Would they want to?

So far, the Goblins seem to be working just fine with the lawful wizards, the Ministry of Magic and whatnot, having even tightened security at Gringotts after Lord Voldemort returned to his body [HBP-6]. The Ministry of Magic has a Goblin Liaison Office [GF-7] (headed, we learn, by one of Slughorn's former students [HBP-4] -- what a surprise). And things seem okay.

It's unclear, however. Maybe they *would* align with Voldemort:

> *"They're not giving anything away yet," said Bill. "I still can't work out whether they believe he's back or not. 'Course, they might prefer not to take sides at all. Keep out of it."*

> *"I'm sure they'd never go over to You-Know-Who," said Mr. Weasley, shaking his head. "They've suffered losses too. Remember that goblin family he murdered last time, somewhere near Nottingham?"*

> *"I think it depends what they're offered," said Lupin. "And I'm not talking about gold; if they're offered freedoms we've been denying them for centuries they're going to be tempted. Have you still not had any luck with Ragnok, Bill?"*

> *"He's feeling pretty anti-wizard at the moment," said Bill. "He hasn't stopped raging about the Bagman business..."* [OP-5]

So... the Goblins might rebel. Or they might not. We've got clues both ways. Love that ambiguity!

Whether the Goblins play a significant role in the plot of Book 7 or not, they do serve an interesting thematic function, as do the House-Elves.

In a sense -- and please *please* don't take me wrong for referring to historic racism here -- the Goblins stand in the place of 19th century (and previous) views of the Jews: They're allowed to live in their own ghettoes and they handle the money. But nothing else is allowed.

(In the same way, although J.K. Rowling isn't writing out of an American tradition, the House-Elves hold much the same position black slaves did in early America: They do the jobs no one else wants to do. Despite their natural talents, they have grossly unequal status in the wizarding world.)

In the end, despite all the set-ups about the Goblins, I doubt the Goblins *will* rebel in book 7. Let's face it, we don't even *know* any goblins. No, I think the Goblins are here as a thematic arrow pointing to the ever-running theme of prejudice. Any greater role they play will only reflect that theme.

CHAPTER 12

THE MOST MAGICAL CREATURE: FAWKES THE PHOENIX

Moving through the set-ups and payoffs surrounding magical creatures in *Harry Potter*, we next come to my favorite magical creature of all: Fawkes.

FAWKES'S POWERS

Phoenixes, of course, have a long, established lore surrounding them, and J.K. Rowling uses much of it in *Harry Potter*, adding to it as well.

Phoenixes burst into flame when it is time for them to die, and are reborn from the ashes. This apparently happens often enough to Fawkes that Dumbledore refers to one of his "burning days" [CS-12].

Dumbledore also tells Harry in *Chamber of Secrets* that phoenixes can carry heavy loads, and that their tears have healing powers. These set-ups are both paid off in the same book, the first when Fawkes's tears heal Harry's fatal wound from the basilisk, saving Harry's life [CS-17], the second when Fawkes carries Harry, Ron, Lockhart and Ginny (easily at least 400 to 450 pounds) out of the Chamber of Secrets [CS-17].

We also see the power of Fawkes's healing tears when he heals the wound Harry got from the spider in the third task of the Triwizard Tournament [GF-38].

But Fawkes, we learn, has the power to heal more than external wounds. His very song provides a deep spiritual comfort and hope. In the graveyard in *Goblet of Fire*, brings Harry hope and somehow conveys to him "Don't break the connection" between his wand and Voldemort's [GF-34].

Later, just one note of Fawkes's song empowers Harry to be able to tell the story of what happened in the graveyard:

> *The phoenix let out one soft, quavering note. It shivered in the air, and Harry felt as though a drop of hot liquid had slipped down his throat into his stomach, warming him, and strengthening him.* [GF-36].

And it is Phoenix Song that magically expresses everyone's grief when Dumbledore dies, and which also empowers them to go forward:

> *Somewhere out in the darkness, a phoenix was singing in a way Harry had never heard before: a stricken lament of terrible beauty. And Harry felt, as he had felt about phoenix song before, that the music was inside him, not without: It was his own grief turned magically to song that echoed across the grounds and through the castle windows.*
>
> *How long they all stood there, listening, he did not know, nor why it seemed to ease their pain a little to listen to the sound of their mourning...* [HBP-29]

In addition, Fawkes (like the House-Elves) can somehow bypass the apparent proscription on Apparating within Hogwarts, and can appear and disappear with ease within the castle [OP-22].

Fawkes is also extraordinarily intelligent. He clearly understands English, delivering messages accurately and responding when Dumbledore tells him, "We will need a warning" [OP-22].

Also, note that it is Fawkes who brings Tom Riddle's diary to Harry when Harry is succumbing to the attack of the basilisk at the end of *Chamber of Secrets* [CS-17]. Harry destroys the diary (which we later learn is a Horcrux containing 1/7 of Voldemort's soul, far more valuable than we could ever have believed during the episode in *Chamber of Secrets*). But Harry couldn't have done so had *Fawkes* not brought it to him. Think: How extremely intelligent must Fawkes be to have known to do that!

Nevertheless, these powers are not the most remarkable thing about Fawkes. No, his most outstanding characteristic is...

FAWKES'S FAITHFULNESS

In *Chamber of Secrets*, Fawkes brings the Sorting Hat (magically concealing Godric Gryffindor's sword) to Harry, thus enabling him to kill the basilisk, *only* after Harry expresses extreme loyalty to Dumbledore [CS-17]. As Dumbledore later tells Harry:

> *"You must have shown me real loyalty down in the Chamber. Nothing but that could have called Fawkes to you."*
> [CS-18]

Fawkes's loyalty extends to throwing himself into harm's way for his "owner" (not quite the right word for his relationship to Dumbledore, but the closest available), or for those loyal to Dumbledore. He saves Harry by attacking the basilisk in the eyes [CS-17]. He swallows the Avada Kedavra curse that Voldemort shoots at Dumbledore in the battle at the Ministry of Magic [OP-36]. His doing so saves Dumbledore's life and kills Fawkes -- but of course, Fawkes immediately is reborn as an ugly baby phoenix.

Fawkes's loyalty to Dumbledore (and vice versa) is understandable. But one little moment shows us that Fawkes has the ability, the free will, as it were, to *choose* whom he aligns himself with: When Harry has to tell the horrible story of Cedric's death and Lord Voldemort's return, Fawkes comes to rest with *Harry* -- *not* with Dumbledore, as one would anticipate -- and gives him the strength to tell the tale.

If Fawkes has the power to choose whom he "belongs" to, where will he land next? We would probably expect him to align himself with Harry, "Dumbledore's man through and through." Harry could certainly use him, and after all, he does have a feather from Fawkes in his wand (although of course, Voldemort does too).

But what if Fawkes goes elsewhere? Who else in our story might also be "Dumbledore's man through and through"?

I do expect the highest probability is that Fawkes will end up with Harry. But what if...

What if Fawkes chose to align himself with Severus Snape?

If Harry is to realize Snape is still on the side of the Order of the *Phoenix*, assuming Snape is in fact his unexpected ally in the war against Voldemort... Could there be a simpler, yet more dramatic way of making that clear than by having Fawkes go to Snape? How could Harry refuse to get that message?

(I am not convinced Harry *will* get that message, as I've said earlier. Snape might have to die for Harry to realize where his true loyalties lie. But if Harry *does* realize it in time, I think there is a very high probability Fawkes will be the messenger.)

Fawkes therefore becomes even more the representative of one of the primary themes of all of *Harry Potter*: the theme of *Loyalty*, brought home especially in *Half-Blood Prince*.

For six books now, we have followed Ron and Hermione's remarkable loyalty to Harry and seen it come to a culmination (so far) in their insistence that they will stick with Harry through Book 7. We have also watched the growth of Harry's astonishing loyalty to Dumbledore, even after death [HBP-30].

And for the last couple of books, at least, we have questioned Snape's loyalty to... whom? *Is* he Dumbledore's man? Or Voldemort's? Or merely his own? The answer to this will be one of the key issues of Book 7.

Fawkes could provide the most economical and trustworthy answer to that crucial question. After all, are we likely to believe *anything* Snape says on the subject? Or anything anyone else says, for that matter? No. But if Fawkes were to show his loyalty to Snape (or conversely, to attack him), we would know clearly where Snape's loyalties *really* lie.

Dumbledore is dead. But I would stake anything that Fawkes did not disappear with him. Fawkes will be back in Book 7, as an aide, as a comforter... and very possibly as a messenger of loyalty.

CHAPTER 13

A GIANT PROBLEM

We have sure spent a lot of time with the giants in the recent *Harry Potter* books.

We've spent chapter after chapter on them, what with Hagrid's and Madame Maxine's unsuccessful trip as Dumbledore's envoys, their near-fruitless attempt to recruit the giants, and Hagrid's return with his half-brother Grawp [OP-20].

Our knowledge of giants, however, is pretty basic. We know they're vicious by nature and hide primarily in mountains abroad [GF-23]. We know they almost killed each other to extinction, with Aurors killing more of them during Voldemort's first reign of terror [GF-23]. We know that the giants who remained joined Voldemort, and that upon his return he immediately planned to call them back [GF-33].

And that's about all we know. Which is really not much for having spent so much time on them. We don't know how they attack wizards or humans in general, except that their recent attacks on Muggles were interpreted by the Muggles as a hurricane [HBP-1]. We don't know how Voldemort manages to wrangle creatures who seem as intent on fighting each other as fighting any enemy. We don't know how many are left or where they are (other than the small band Hagrid found -- and we don't know where *they* are, either).

We do know there's at least one giant in England (besides Grawp). Are there more? We simply don't know. (And by the way, why is it so hard for the Ministry of Magic to find this giant? Shouldn't he be pretty easy to spot?)

Even the time we've spent with Hagrid and Grawp doesn't illuminate us much. Grawp can clearly be somewhat domesticated, as we see at Dumbledore's funeral, where he's wearing normal clothes and (quite sweetly) trying to comfort his "big" brother [HBP-30]. But from what we can see, he doesn't seem to have come *that* far along from when he was grunting "Hermy" and pulling down trees for fun. (Clearly in giant-wizard matches, the wizard strain of DNA is extremely dominant, if we compare the half-giants Madame Maxime and Hagrid to Grawp and the other giants we've met.)

So *why* have we spent so much time on them? Was it all just so Grawp could scare off the centaurs and save Harry and Hermione in the Forbidden Forest [OP-33]? That's an awful lot of set-up for really not much payoff at all.

Or was it yet again to give us another expression of the theme of prejudice? Dumbledore says as much when he tells Fudge to send envoys to the giants:

> *"The second step you must take-- and at once," Dumbledore pressed on, "is to send envoys to the giants."*
>
> *"Envoys to the giants?" Fudge shrieked, finding his tongue again. "What madness is this?"*
>
> *"Extend them the hand of friendship, now, before it is too late," said Dumbledore, "or Voldemort will persuade them, as he did before, that he alone among wizards will give them their rights and their freedom!"*

"You -- you cannot be serious!" Fudge gasped, shaking his head and retreating further from Dumbledore. "If the magical community got wind that I had approached the giants -- people hate them, Dumbledore -- end of my career--"

"You are blinded," said Dumbledore, his voice rising now, the aura of power around him palpable, his eyes blazing once more, "by the love of the office you hold, Cornelius! You place too much importance, and you always have done, on the so-called purity of blood! You fail to recognize that it matters not what someone is born, but what they grow to be!" [GF-36]

So what are we to make of this massive amount of set-up, with virtually no payoff showing up as yet?

I see three possibilities: (1) We will come back to the giants as part of the wrap-up of Hagrid's story; *or* (2) Voldemort will incorporate the giants (plural, not just the one roaming around Britain at the present) as part of his army of dementors, inferi, Death Eaters and other unsavory types, and we will see (or hear about) some major destruction; *or* (3) the giant storyline is in part what J.K. Rowling was referring to when she said that she had overwritten Book 5 and should have cut down some parts of the story.

My bet is choice no. 3. We've had a lot of set-up about those giants, but for my money, they haven't been that illuminating even to our understanding of Hagrid's part of the story, and I think they're really a plot and thematic device that got a little out of hand.

But I certainly could be wrong -- because the set-ups are there.

CHAPTER 14

MAGICAL CREATURES GALORE

There sure are a lot of Magical Creatures in *Harry Potter*. Let's run through a few more who have some intriguing set-ups.

CENTAURS

Centaurs are smarter than humans [OP-33]. That's made quite clear to us... by the centaurs. Which raises the question: Are they *really* smarter than humans? Or are we seeing a reverse prejudice? (After all, they were certainly fooled by an underage witch pretty easily.)

In any event, centaurs definitely don't acknowledge any possibility of wizard superiority, nor do they acknowledge wizard laws [OP-33]. They certainly don't want to be manipulated by wizards [OP-33]. In fact, as far as they're concerned, in spite of the fact that it stands on Hogwarts grounds, even the Forbidden Forest belongs to them [OP-33].

This helps us understand (if not condone) the centaur reaction to Firenze. Firenze has been able to look beyond his kind's prejudice from the beginning, when he allied with humans against "what is lurking in this forest" [SS-15]. He thus stands in contrast to, say, Bane, who keeps his prejudice against humans intact. In fact, Firenze is banished from the forest precisely *because* he steps past this prejudice to work for Dumbledore [OP-27].

Firenze pays a steep price for his open-mindedness. The centaurs refuse to forgive him for his betrayal, so much so that Hagrid has to stop them from killing Firenze [OP-30].

Will we see a payoff for all this prejudice? I doubt that we'll actually see much more about the centaurs, because it's unlikely we'll be at Hogwarts much in Book 7. But I could be wrong: We have a lot of wizards-prejudiced-against-other-creatures story lines going on (House-Elves, Giants, etc.), and the centaurs are the only creatures we've seen who are prejudiced against wizards, making it a particularly interesting way to explore the theme. However -- how much time will we have in Book 7 to focus just on theme, given all the plot to be covered?

One last thing about the centaurs: What about their ability to foretell the future? It might be nice to get a little payoff there.

But given the extreme vagueness of the centaurs' predictions, would more predictions do us that much good? Let's face it, it's not even clear whether the "calm between two great wars" [OP-27] refers to the calm between Voldemort's first attempt to take power and his second, or between the WWII era battle against Grindelwald and the rise of Voldemort.

WEREWOLVES

Other than the understanding we develop for Remus Lupin, we really don't know or hear that much about werewolves until *Half-Blood Prince*.

But boy, do those werewolves come out of the woodwork then! We learn for the first time that there are a lot of them around, and that Lupin is living with them, trying to win them to the good side of the battle against Voldemort [HBP-16]. We also learn the werewolves tend to side with Voldemort, because they know he can offer them a better life [HBP-16]. Given the werewolves' predilections, it seems likely that Voldemort will deliver on this offer.

Most of our expanded knowledge of werewolves, however, focuses on one werewolf in particular: Fenrir Greyback.

Fenrir, we learn, revels in being a werewolf. He considers it his mission to contaminate as many wizards as possible [HBP-16], specializing in children, whom he hopes to train to hate wizards. To that end, he positions himself near his victims as the full moon approaches, the better to attack once he has transformed [HBP-16]. And, as when he attacks Bill Weasley, he will even attack (with less than complete results) when it's *not* a full moon [HBP-29].

Voldemort is deploying Fenrir well, it seems. He uses Fenrir as a threat against people's children [HBP-16]. And he follows through on that threat at least once in *Half-Blood Prince*, with the Montgomery son attacked when his mother refused to help Voldemort [HBP-22]. Fenrir is treated as a trusted lieutenant, apparently, given that he hangs with esteemed purebred families such as the Malfoys [HBP-17].

But Fenrir is unpredictable. Although it's repeated often during the final battle at Hogwarts in *Half-Blood Prince* that Harry must be saved for Voldemort, Fenrir attacks him -- possibly against Voldemort's express orders [HBP-28].

So as we head for Book 7, we have a dangerous, uncontrollable werewolf on the loose. We spent so much time hearing about him in Book 6, I definitely think Fenrir's story is not over. I don't think such a powerful character would be introduced just to savage Bill Weasley and disappear. Will he play a major role in Book 7, or just be a distraction from the bigger battle, an obstacle to overcome, as it were? I would guess the latter, but I do think we'll see him again.

We're not done contemplating werewolves... but we'll hold off on further discussion until Chapter 32.

DRAGONS

It would be nice to see some dragons again. But given that, outside the Triwizard Tournament, all we've been told about them is that there are two types native to Britain [SS-14], and given that we've been given no set-up to see more of Charlie Weasley, I sort of doubt it.

Sigh. Wouldn't a dragon battle be fun, though?

OWLS

We've seen so much of owls throughout *Harry Potter* that we sort of take them for granted. But there's one big, gigantic set-up we've been handed as almost a throwaway.

We see it clearly when Sirius Black is in hiding, and Harry uses a school owl, rather than Hedwig, to find him [GF-18]. This indicates something important: *Any owl can find any wizard.*

Think about that. If any owl can find any wizard, then could an owl find Voldemort?

The answer to this depends on the answer to another question: If a wizard makes his location Unplottable, does that spell affect animals? Given how well Sirius was hidden, with random owls still able to find him, I'm guessing the answer to *this* question is no.

But what good will it do, you ask, if the owl can't communicate Voldemort's location back to Harry? Well, we've heard Harry say quite a few times that he prefers flying to Apparating. What if Harry followed, say, Hedwig on her voyage toward Voldemort?

If Voldemort hides from Harry and Harry has to find him, we've been given a beautiful, clean, elegant way for Harry to do just that.

VAMPIRES

We finally see a vampire in *Half-Blood Prince*, when Sanguini (what a great name!) makes his appearance at Slughorn's Christmas party [HBP-15]. Sanguini is almost a comic character here, certainly not a scary one, so I do think he's here mainly for color and a bit of comic relief. I don't think we'll see him or any other vampires again.

However, I think Sanguini's presence accomplishes what we might think of as a "meta-purpose": He makes it clear that Severus Snape is not, as many have opined, a vampire or a half-vampire (something J.K. Rowling has confirmed in interviews as well). Now that we see what vampires are like in Rowling's universe, they are as far from Snape in personality as possible -- hopefully putting the question to rest.

VEELA

We will certainly see Veela again, given that Fleur's relatives are likely to attend her wedding.

Raising the question: What powers does Fleur have (other

than making Ron do foolish things)? Will she turn into one of those birdlike monsters [GF-8] to defend Bill or others? Because, let's face it, do we really think that wedding will come off without some Death Eaters making an appearance?

So my bet is, yes, we will see Fleur in action.

OTHER MAGICAL CREATURES

Plenty of other magical creatures are mentioned -- Chameleon Ghouls [CS-11], Blood-sucking Bugbears [CS-11] and the like. And once we add in *Fantastic Beasts and Where to Find Them*, we've got lots to draw from. But Rowling has said she won't be introducing new characters for the most part in Book 7 -- and I feel that includes new monsters. I think we've seen all the Fantastic Beasts we're going to see.

So let's leave the wide-ranging topic of Magical Creatures and move on to Magical Objects.

CHAPTER 15

MAGICAL OBJECTS: WEASLEY'S WIZARD WHEEZES

We run into lots of fun (and sometimes scary) magical objects in *Harry Potter,* and we've certainly seen through the first six books how well they can be set up for future payoff (as witness the Vanishing Cabinet).

Let's take a look at some of the magical objects we may see again in Book 7, starting with Fred and George's inventions.

Fred and George Weasley are deceptively talented wizards, and have been so from an early age. Ron tells us that when he was 5-years-old (meaning when the twins were approximately 7), they turned his teddy bear into a spider [CS-9] -- pretty impressive magic when we know that many young wizards haven't produced any magic whatsoever at that age.

Even Hermione, a pretty tough witch to impress, *is* impressed by the twins' magic, against her own best instincts. She admits that the Headless Hats, which extend their reach of invisibility past the actual object, are so clever she can't figure them out [OP-24]. Moreover, Hermione calls their Daydream charms "extraordinary magic" [HBP-6]. And let's not forget that Flitwick thought their Portable Swamp [OP-29] was terrific magic as well.

But all that magic being produced for fun can have, as we have already seen, a darker application. Draco Malfoy uses the twins' Peruvian Instant Darkness Powder [HBP-6] as a key ingredient in his plan to let Death Eaters into Hogwarts -- and like most of the twins' inventions, it works all too well:

> *"--Peruvian Instant Darkness Powder,"* said Ron bitterly. *"Fred and George's. I'm going to be having a word with them about who they let buy their products."* [HBP-29]

Ron's point is well-taken indeed. Fred and George's products work *too* well in the wrong hands. So let's take a look at the rest of their inventions (that we know of), and think about how they could be used in Book 7.

--Canary Creams [GF-21] -- It's hard to see candy that turns the eater into a giant canary being used for more than fun.

--Extendable Ears [OP-4] -- A very useful invention already, but not one that Fred and George have made available to the public. We probably won't need them to spy on the Order of the Phoenix, since our main players will be of age in Book 7 -- but we could use them for standard spying as the trio did at Borgin and Burkes.

--Skiving Snackboxes [OP-17] -- A little too Hogwarts-specific, perhaps, to be needed in Book 7. But you never know...

--Weasleys' Wizard Whiz-Bangs [OP-28] -- Frankly, I wouldn't be surprised to see these again in *Movie* 7, whether they appear in Book 7 or not. Fireworks -- especially of such a spectacular nature -- are always worth looking at! Useful for the plot? Probably not. But maybe we'll see them in celebration at the end of the book?

--Punching telescope [HBP-5] -- Given that this item was such a throwaway, and that it was deemed unfinished by the twins, I wouldn't be surprised at all to see it show up in Book 7.

--Bruise remover [HBP-6] -- A handy thing to have, but probably not a player in any future plotting.

--Edible Dark Marks [HBP-6] -- These are cute, and clever in that they help wizards make fun of the Dark Lord (a good way to subtly weaken his power). They make me wonder if the twins might not go further in this direction -- could they create a faux (yet functional) Dark Mark if someone needed to go undercover? I bet they could.

--Magic quills (self-inking, spell-checking, smart-answer) [HBP-6] -- Again, a little too Hogwarts-specific for any future plot, I think. Although I do wonder just which meaning the twins ascribe to "spell-checking"?

--Reusable Hangman [HBP-6] -- I trust Mattel is paying attention to this one!

--Wonder Witch love potions [HBP-6] -- As discussed in Chapter 2, we've already seen some payoff to these, with Romilda Vane going after Harry and ending up with Ron. We've also seen how crafty Fred and George are even in their marketing, disguising these contraband items as perfume and cough syrup [HBP-15]. I wonder if the love potion episode with Harry was in itself a bit of a set-up: We now have in our minds the idea that Fred and George's items can be used against Harry. Which should make us think: What *else* of the twins' could be used against Harry?

--Shield Hats, Cloaks and Gloves [HBP-6] -- Now *these* are useful! And with the Ministry of Magic already ordering them, I'm expecting that we will indeed see them in use (probably not by the trio) in Book 7. Can't you just see Cornelius Fudge in complete Shield regalia?

--Decoy Detonators [HBP-6] -- A clever invention. And Fred

and George already handed a bunch to Harry. Hey, if *I* had a handful of these stuffed in my trunk, *I'd* sure use them.

--Pygmy Puffs [HBP-6] -- Just cute, I think. Although we could see something sad happen to Ginny's pet, I suppose.

And let's not forget:

-U-No-Poo [HBP-6] -- One of the biggest laughs of *Half-Blood Prince*, right up there with Luna commenting on Quidditch. But it's a one-time-only laugh, I think. Look to see a similar funny invention -- but not U-No-Poo again.

This list covers the bulk of Fred and George's inventions. But who knows what they've invented between books?

I expect to see something glorious from the twins in Book 7. The moment where they stood up to Umbridge in *Order of the Phoenix* was, for my money, one of the best of all the books. With J.K. Rowling's recent statement that two characters will die in Book 7 whom she didn't expect to die, I admit my inner Molly Weasley is worried for Fred and George. But if they should die, at the very least, they deserve to go out in extreme glory!

CHAPTER 16

MORE MAGICAL OBJECTS

DARK OBJECTS HIDDEN AT THE MALFOYS'

Apparently Lucius Malfoy has quite the treasure trove of dark objects hidden away at his manor. In *Chamber of Secrets*, he sells some of his goodies to Borgin at Borgin and Burkes in order to avoid a Ministry of Magic inquiry -- but we learn he has more sequestered away [CS-4]. Later Draco tells "Crabbe" and "Goyle" (actually Harry and Ron under the influence of Polyjuice Potion) that his father has dark objects hidden away in secret in a chamber under their drawing room floor [CS-12].

Several books later, after the acknowledged return of Voldemort and the revelation that Lucius was on the Dark Lord's side, the Ministry of Magic belatedly raids the Malfoy home, but doesn't get much, though Arthur Weasley *thinks* they got everything dangerous [HBP-7]. Harry, obsessed with Draco, pushes Arthur to go back again. Arthur does so, but finds nothing further [HBP-11].

But it's important to note that the Malfoys held in their possession one of *the* most valuable dark objects on the face of the earth: Tom Riddle's diary [CS-18], which, we learn much later, actually contained one-seventh of Voldemort's soul:

> "...*Of course, Lucius did not know what the diary really was. I understand that Voldemort had told him the diary would*

cause the Chamber of Secrets to reopen because it was cleverly enchanted. Had Lucius known he held a portion of his master's soul in his hands, he would undoubtedly have treated it with more reverence -- but instead he went ahead and carried out the old plan for his own ends: By planting the diary upon Arthur Weasley's daughter, he hoped to discredit Arthur and get rid of a highly incriminating magical object in one stroke..." [HBP-23]

What else does Lucius have hidden away? (Let's face it: Do we really believe that Arthur, sweet as he is, couldn't be fooled by the devious Lucius Malfoy into missing some hidden items?) Specifically, does he have another Horcrux?

I don't think it would have been good planning on Voldemort's part to have two Horcruxes stored in the same location (not just because of potential treachery -- what if there was, say, a fire?).

But I don't think we've seen everything the Malfoys have at their disposal. Draco's storyline has a long way to go, and he has been quite busy indeed with dark objects -- the Vanishing Cabinet, the Hand of Glory, the Peruvian Darkness Powder (not a Dark Object per se, but certainly used for dark means). I think we will see more of what's hidden in that chamber under the drawing room.

THE PENSIEVE

We've gotten some good use out of Dumbledore's Pensieve -- and so has J.K. Rowling! What a wonderful creation for a writer to have in her back pocket -- a magical device that allows all sorts of flashbacks and exposition that would otherwise have to be explained in interminable dialogue.

Harry found out what the Pensieve does by mistake (or

through an overabundance of curiosity) when he "fell" into Dumbledore's memories regarding Barty Crouch [GF-30].

The Pensieve makes another appearance in *Order of the Phoenix* when Snape uses it to store his more vulnerable memories during Occlumency lessons [OP-28] -- with Harry, again showing too much curiosity, learning more about "Snape's Worst Memory" than the Potions Master would have wished him to know.

But the Pensieve really comes into its own in *Half-Blood Prince* when Dumbledore uses it to take Harry (and us) through his research about Tom Riddle, and when Slughorn provides his own memory of his conversation with Riddle about Horcruxes.

The Pensieve has served us well, and we really don't *have* to see it again in Book 7. But shouldn't Harry think about it somewhere during his quest for the Horcruxes?

Rowling has confirmed that the Pensieve shows what *really* happened in the past, not one's faulty memory of what happened. That being the case, it would seem that if Harry *really* wants to know what happened at Godric's Hollow, he might learn more by visiting the Pensieve than by visiting the village itself.

After all, he was there the night Voldemort killed his parents. We've seen his flashes of memory of that horrible night. What if the rest of the memories are resting in his brain, just waiting to be unlocked in the Pensieve?

One caveat: It's possible that Harry *won't* be able to use the Pensieve to recover those memories. After all, the memory of his parents' death wasn't enough to allow him to see the Thestrals; it took Cedric's death (and time for it to sink in) to allow that to happen [OP-21].

It's conceivable that the Pensieve works the same way, that it won't allow memories to be recovered that occurred before a certain age or level of awareness.

But I sure think it's worth it for Harry to give it a try. And if Harry does indeed refuse to go back to Hogwarts at the beginning of Book 7, and Rowling needs a way to get him there, a visit to retrieve the Pensieve would be a good reason indeed.

THE HEADMASTER PORTRAITS

The portraits of past Headmasters in the Headmaster's office at Hogwarts seem to have a few magical properties that other wizarding portraits do not have. Not only can the Headmasters move between pictures at Hogwarts, but they are able to move between the portraits of themselves in different locations, as well as between the pictures in any of *those* locations [OP-22].

And while the Headmasters seem to spend most of their time sleeping [CS-12] (they are, after all, all dead -- and most likely quite old on top of that), they do listen to what goes on in the Headmaster's office [OP-22].

Moreover, these reflections of the former Headmasters are required to serve the current Headmaster:

"We are honor-bound to give service to the present Headmaster of Hogwarts!" cried a frail-looking old wizard whom Harry recognized as Dumbledore's predecessor, Armando Dippet. [OP-22]

This service can involve running errands, as when Dumbledore asks two former Heads to go to the Ministry of Magic and St. Mungo's and report back what's happening [OP-22], or when he has the reluctant Phineas Nigellus convey a message to Sirius [OP-22].

What's interesting to me is that not only do the former Headmasters do what the Headmaster asks, but they seem to have a real loyalty to him. All the Headmaster portraits witness what happens when Dumbledore hexes Umbridge, Fudge, et al., then disappears with Fawkes. Yet none of them turns Dumbledore in, not even Phineas Nigellus whom one would think would have no personal reason to side with Dumbledore (coming from the Black family as he does) [OP-27].

But we're not likely to spend much time at Hogwarts in Book 7. So why does it matter what the Headmaster portraits can and can't do? Well, it matters because of the new portrait just added: that of Dumbledore himself [HBP-29].

How much of his living past can a portrait remember? Can Dumbledore's portrait convey to Harry all the other clues and hints about the Horcruxes that Harry never got to hear? Can he finally tell Harry the story of how his hand was destroyed?

We don't have much idea how to answer these questions -- but I think they *must* be answered in Book 7, given the prominence of the mention of Dumbledore's portrait. Now maybe Harry won't think to go ask the portrait until it's too late (as he forgot the Two-Way Mirror). Or maybe his access to Hogwarts will be blocked. I believe, however, that this is a set-up that *must* be paid off.

THE WEASLEYS' CLOCK

Sigh. I really hope that some of the problems with the Weasley's clock are problems that came up in editing, or even are problems specific to the U.S. edition.

Problems, you ask? What problems? Well...

When we first see the one-of-a-kind clock, it only has one hand, which points to things like "Time to make tea" or "Time to feed the chickens" or "You're late" [CS-3].

When we next see the clock (and the phrasing makes it seem as if we're discussing the same clock Harry saw on an earlier visit to the Burrow), it's specified that it's a grandfather clock. The clock now has one hand for each member of the family, pointing to the location or condition of that person (home, work, school, traveling, lost, hospital, prison, mortal peril) [GF-10]. It's this version of the clock that Dumbledore speaks of so approvingly in *Order of the Phoenix* [OP-22].

But when we go back to the clock in *Half-Blood Prince*, it still reflects the location/condition of the family members (all at "mortal peril," however, which seems less than useful) [HBP-6]. But now, Molly Weasley is able to carry it around and prop it in her laundry basket [HBP-5]. Awfully hard to do that with a grandfather clock.

Oops.

Since we're going back to the Burrow for Bill and Fleur's wedding, I do hope to see the clock again. I'd like to know if Fleur's name gets magically added when she marries Bill. I'd also like to see (well, not really) if someone's name disappears from the clock if they die. Also, given the special position Harry holds in Molly's heart, as discussed in Chapter 6, I wouldn't be surprised to see Harry's name up on the clock by the end of Book 7.

BROOMSTICKS

We see a lot of broomsticks throughout the books, of course, and my interest here isn't to discuss the relative quality of the Nimbus 2000 vs. the Firebolt. I'll leave that to the hard-core Quidditch fans.

I just want to note how incredibly great Harry is on a broom. He's a natural. He can fly like a pro without taking a single lesson, indeed, without ever having set, um, butt on a broom before [SS-9]. Even McGonagall is astonished:

> *"The boy's a natural. I've never seen anything like it.... He caught that thing in his hand after a fifty-foot dive," Professor McGonagall told Wood. "Didn't even scratch himself. Charlie Weasley couldn't have done it."* [SS-9]

We've seen payoffs already for Harry's remarkable flying ability, of course, on the Quidditch field, and most impressively, in the first task of the Triwizard Tournament.

But I wouldn't be surprised to see Harry do some seriously important flying in Book 7. We're reminded several times in *Half-Blood Prince* that Harry prefers flying to Apparition [HBP-18]. I've already suggested that possibly Harry could find Voldemort, should he need to, by *flying* after an owl.

And there's this little nugget dropped for apparently no reason by Hagrid at Harry's first Quidditch match: Only powerful Dark Magic can interfere with a broom [SS-11].

Why would we need to know that? Could Harry's flying be in for some interference in Book 7?

We know there'll be no Quidditch in Book 7. But I doubt that means there'll be no flying.

CHAPTER 17

MAGICAL OBJECTS GALORE

Let's flash through the rest of the Magical Objects of interest, so we can move away from things and back to people in our next chapter.

DRAGON'S BLOOD

Dumbledore was the one who discovered the twelve uses of dragon's blood [SS-6]. But we only see it used once: When Slughorn splatters it on the walls of the house he's squatting in to fool Dumbledore into thinking he's dead [HBP-4]. One has to wonder, given the expense of dragon's blood [HBP-4], why Slughorn used *it* rather than some other sort of random blood. Was it just to remind us that it's out there?

Also, somehow I doubt that one of Dumbledore's twelve stated uses was to splatter it on the walls to make people think you're dead. (Just guessing here.) So what are the other twelve uses? Will they come into play in Book 7? I actually think they could, given all the emphasis on Potions in *Half-Blood Prince*, especially the extreme stress on how Lily was so good at Potions. Not necessary, but if it shows up, it's certainly been set-up. (And perhaps Portrait-Dumbledore will be able to chat about those twelve uses if need be...)

SNEAKOSCOPES

Sneakoscopes seem to be so very sensitive, one has to wonder if they're really all that useful. Harry's "pocket" Sneakoscope (are there different sizes, by the way?), a gift from Ron in *Prisoner of Azkaban* [PA-1], won't stop spinning and lighting up, both on the train [PA-5] and when it breaks loose from its confinement in their dorm room [PA-11]. And Fake-Moody has actually disabled his Sneakoscope because, he claims, it's so sensitive [GF-20].

But with all their annoying properties, it's clear that Sneakoscopes definitely work, despite Bill Weasley's failure to take them seriously [PA-1]. Harry's only goes crazy when Scabbers is around [PA-5, 11] -- and *he's* certainly untrustworthy. And forget what Fake-Moody says about students lying about their homework -- the *real* reason his Sneakoscope wouldn't shut up has to be because he wasn't Mad-Eye Moody at all!

We've been dragging that Sneakoscope around for a long time without using it. Maybe Harry will think to put it to use in Book 7. Wouldn't it be interesting to pull it out around Snape, for instance?

THE TWO-WAY MIRROR

Some people give great gifts, and Sirius Black was clearly one of them. Yes, he absolutely should have told Harry what the Two-Way Mirror was when he gave it to him in *Order of the Phoenix* [OP-24] -- though of course he had no way of knowing Harry wouldn't open the present. (Silly Harry. Let this be a lesson to us all: Always open your Christmas presents!)

We finally learn what a great gift it could have been when Harry opens it after Sirius's death and reads the note:

"This is a two-way mirror. I've got the other. If you need to speak to me, just say my name into it; you'll appear in my mirror and I'll be able to talk in yours. James and I used to use them when we were in separate detentions." [OP-38]

Harry thinks it's worthless after he tries to talk to the now-dead Sirius with it, and can't. (Note, by the way, how this plot beat underlines J.K. Rowling's oft-stated point that death is final and not reversible by magic.) Understandably angry, Harry throws the Two-Way Mirror into his trunk and it shatters [OP-38].

We know we *will* see the two-way mirror again. Rowling practically promised us this in an interview. And since we didn't see it in *Half-Blood Prince*, that means we've got to see it in Book 7.

"But Harry shattered it!" I hear you exclaim. Yes, but isn't it convenient that he shattered it *in his trunk*. Given the pigsty that is Harry's trunk, my bet is the pieces are still rattling around in there, ready for Hermione to slap a nice *Reparo* spell on them.

As for the other half of the Mirror -- well, if it went through the veil with Sirius, of course it's now unreachable. But would Sirius really have carried it on his person when he was essentially under house arrest? My bet is that when Harry goes to 12, Grimmauld Place, he'll find Mirror #2 waiting for him. And I'm thinking these visual walkie-talkies, as it were, will be quite handy indeed in Book 7.

THE HAND OF GLORY

I think we've seen the payoff for this already in *Half-Blood Prince*. But what a nice set-up it was, really a throwaway:

"Ah, the Hand of Glory!" said Mr. Borgin, abandoning Mr. Malfoy's list and scurrying over to Draco. "Insert a candle

and it gives light only to the holder! Best friend of thieves and plunderers! Your son has fine taste, sir."

"I hope my son will amount to more than a thief or a plunderer, Borgin," said Mr. Malfoy coldly... [CS-4]

Over 2500 pages (and six years) between set-up and payoff. Props to Rowling on this one!

THE SORTING HAT

Yes, the Sorting Hat belonged to Godric Gryffindor, and yes, Harry is looking for a Horcrux that may have come from Gryffindor... But I don't think it's the Sorting Hat, for one very good reason.

The Hat can talk. And as we see in its song in *Order of the Phoenix* [OP-11], it has a mind of its own. Do we really think it would allow itself to have part of Voldemort's soul sequestered away inside it and not mention it to anyone? I don't.

I'm most interested in the Sorting Hat's ability to read minds. It certainly knows what Harry is thinking when he's Sorted [SS-7]. And it remembers it a year later. If we had access to the Hat in Book 7, could we possibly use it as a form of Legilimency? A long shot, I think, but possible.

THE MARAUDER'S MAP

Again, I think the Marauder's Map, like the Hand of Glory, has done all it really can do for us. It's helped Harry in and out of a myriad of sneaking-around situations, it's given him a link to his father, it's helped confuse us all regarding Fake-Moody/Barty Crouch Jr. (and given us helpful clues, had we remembered Lupin's statement that "The Marauder's Map never lies" [PA-18]).

But I don't think we'll get much more out of it, especially if we're spending little time at Hogwarts in Book 7. A marvelous Magical Object, though, and one that has given us a lot of great payoffs.

MAGIC CARPETS

These are banned in Britain because they're "Muggle artifacts" [GF-7] (but isn't a broom equally a "Muggle artifact"? Just asking). Given Harry's preference for flying compared to Apparition, and given the probable need for our trio to get places together quickly, we could possibly see magic carpets in Book 7. (Although probably they will just Apparate.) Not a prediction, just a possibility.

OMNIOCULARS

Someone in the Muggle world has to be working on these right now -- just combine Tivo with binoculars, and you've got Omnioculars. (And I'll buy a set!)...

The Omnioculars have to be of more use than just watching Quidditch matches [GF-7], and could serve as the visual equivalent of Extendable Ears -- if Harry and Ron can remember they have them when they need them for spying.

DARK DETECTORS

Fake-Moody has a whole raft of cool instruments in *Goblet of Fire*: Secrecy Sensors, a Foe-Glass, and lots of other unexplained items [GF-20]. It makes me wonder: What else do Aurors have available to them? And could our trio get their hands on some of it?

DUMBLEDORE'S INSTRUMENTS

Fake-Moody isn't the only professor with cool stuff in his office. Harry sees plenty of unexplained magical objects when he first enters Dumbledore's office:

> *A number of curious silver instruments stood on spindle-legged tables, whirring and emitting little puffs of smoke.* [CS-12]

What do they all do? Well, we only learn what one does -- and we don't learn all that much. Dumbledore uses one of the instruments to determine something enigmatic regarding Nagini after Mr. Weasley is bitten [OP-22]. (I personally think he was using the instrument to determine whether Nagini was a Horcrux.)

What else are they good for? Does McGonagall know (if she's even confirmed as Headmistress, which I don't think is a given)? Can Portrait-Dumbledore explain them? Will Harry have access to them? Will they still work with Dumbledore dead?

Or are they just cool items we will never see again, because to give Harry too many answers too easily would be, well, too easy?

SIRIUS'S MOTORCYCLE

Sirius's flying motorcycle is a cool magical object, set up at the *very* beginning of the story when Hagrid shows up at 4, Privet Drive with baby Harry [SS-1].

Could we see it again? Notice that Rowling goes out of her way to have Kingsley Shacklebolt bring it up in Harry's hearing [OP-7]. Since we always want to pay attention when Rowling makes a point of mentioning something a second time for no seeming reason, my guess is yes, we will see it again.

Where is it? If Sirius can keep a hippogriff indoors, why wouldn't he keep a motorcycle inside, too? I think it's still at 12, Grimmauld Place, waiting for Harry, who we know would rather fly than apparate. Wouldn't it be a nice visual "step-into-manhood" to see him mount his godfather's motorcycle?

TIME TURNERS

We have definitely seen the last of these. Hermione reminds us in *Half-Blood Prince* that they were all smashed to bits in the Battle at the Ministry of Magic.

An important line, as it guarantees we can't just say "Hey, let's get a time-turner and go back to before Dumbledore was killed!" And I'm glad, as to have the ability to manipulate time would really detract from the playing out of Harry's story.

CHAPTER 18

SLUGHORN THE WEAK

As the official "visiting professor" of Book 6, Horace Slughorn stands a very good chance of reappearing in Book 7. After all, we have had at least a token re-appearance from all our previous visiting professors except poor Professor Quirrell, who ended Book 1 a bit, um, indisposed.

So what set-ups have we been given about Slughorn, and what role is he likely to play in Book 7?

The overriding characteristic of Slughorn is his weakness. He is weak in the sense of being prone to manipulation (both as the manipulator and the manipulated). Weak in his always protecting himself, of having the instinct to hide and lie. Weak in that he typically tries to ride the coattails of power, and to impress others by his proximity to power.

Slughorn is a wonderfully apt character for our own celebrity-driven culture. We recognize him immediately -- and to our shame, often recognize pieces of him in ourselves.

Let's look at specifics. For once, instead of having to figure out the truth about a visiting professor, Dumbledore tells Harry (and us) exactly what Slughorn is about from the get-go:

"Horace," said Dumbledore... "likes his comfort. He also

likes the company of the famous, the successful, and the powerful. He enjoys the feeling that he influences these people. He has never wanted to occupy the throne himself; he prefers the back seat -- more room to spread out, you see. He used to handpick favorites at Hogwarts, sometimes for their ambition or their brains, sometimes for their charm or their talent, and he had an uncanny knack for choosing those who would go on to become outstanding in their various fields. Horace formed a kind of club of his favorites with himself at the center, making introductions, forging useful contacts between members, and always reaping some kind of benefit in return, whether a free box of his favorite crystalized pineapple or the chance to recommend the next junior member of the Goblin Liaison Office."

Harry had a sudden and vivid mental image of a great swollen spider, spinning a web around it, twitching a thread here and there to bring its large and juicy flies a little closer.

"I tell you all this," Dumbledore continued, "not to turn you against Horace -- or, as we must now call him, Professor Slughorn -- but to put you on your guard. He will undoubtedly try to collect you, Harry. You would be the jewel of his collection; 'the Boy Who Lived'... or, as they call you these days, 'the Chosen One.'" [HBP-4]

Notice that Dumbledore isn't warning Harry because he thinks Harry is in danger from Slughorn. He is warning Harry against letting himself be manipulated -- a warning that will stand Harry in good stead against others, for instance, as Rufus Scrimgeour moves in on him.

Slughorn, of course, as a master manipulator, recognizes Harry's attempted (and clumsy) manipulation easily, when Harry first goes after Slughorn's untampered-with memory [HBP-17].

It's to Slughorn's credit that he is genuinely ashamed of having given Tom Riddle such detailed information about Horcruxes [HBP-22]. When we see the memory, we get the sense that Slughorn regretted giving out the information even as he was doing it [HBP-23]. And he gives Harry that memory -- at least in part -- out of his love for the memory of Lily Evans (with yet another reminder of Harry having "his mother's eyes") [HBP-22].

However, even as we see a sense of morality, a sense of knowing right from wrong lying deep within Slughorn, we see his abiding weakness: Yes, he does the right thing and gives Harry the memory -- but his overriding concern is what Harry thinks of him [HBP-21]. And yes, he gave Harry the memory out of his love of Lily -- but also because Harry appeals to his hunger for power-proximity when he says that, yes, he *is* the 'Chosen One' [HBP-22].

Again, when Dumbledore is killed, Slughorn's shock and dismay seem entirely genuine -- but his weakness shows through in that his first thoughts are of himself:

> *"Snape!" ejaculated Slughorn, who looked the most shaken,*
> *pale and sweating. "Snape! I taught him! I thought I knew him!"*
> [HBP-29]

Now for the big question: Is Slughorn a secret Death Eater?

I don't think so. I don't think someone this in love with what we might call "earthly" power would ever take sides that definitively. It's not in his character to do so.

Siding with Voldemort would in fact mean an end to all the favor-currying Slughorn practices so assiduously; it would mean an end to his lifestyle. Yes, Voldemort can promise to provide a certain kind of power: power to destroy. But this is *not* the kind of power Slughorn craves.

In fact, when Slughorn starts to revive the "Slug Club" upon his return to Hogwarts, he *avoids* recruiting students with ties to the Death Eaters [HBP-7]. He also lies (not a surprise) when Harry asks him about Horcruxes, specifically out of fear of being linked to the Dark Lord [HBP-18].

No, if Slughorn is evil, it is not because he has chosen what is wrong in lieu of what is right. It is because he has made the choice "between what is right and what is easy" [GF-37] -- and has come down squarely on the "easy" side of the equation.

So why do I think Slughorn will make an appearance in Book 7?

Slughorn is just too important to Voldemort for us not to see him again. Dumbledore acknowledges that Slughorn has "considerable skills" that the Death Eaters would find useful [HBP-4] (Among them, we learn, is Occlumency [HBP-17]). But I don't think this is the real reason Slughorn is on the run from Voldemort when we first meet him.

Slughorn is valuable to Lord Voldemort because he is one of the few people left alive who knew him as Tom Riddle. And, with Dumbledore dead, he is one of the *extremely* few people alive (four, by my count) who know Voldemort has been making Horcruxes [HBP-19].

In short, Voldemort has very good reason to recruit Slughorn -- not to use his talents, but because he wants (a) to know whom Slughorn has told about his Horcrux conversation with Tom Riddle and (b) to kill him.

So not only do I think we will see Slughorn in Book 7, but I think we will see him safely holed up at Hogwarts (assuming Hogwarts is still a safe place to be), probably as head of Slytherin house. And I doubt he will set foot outside the castle until Voldemort is vanquished.

A true Slytherin, that Horace.

CHAPTER 19

UNLIKELY GRYFFINDORS

On the list of Gryffindors, we find two unlikely housemates: Neville Longbottom and Percy Weasley.

NEVILLE LONGBOTTOM

I actually expected a lot more from Neville in *Half-Blood Prince*. I wanted to see him be a true Gryffindor, I wanted to see him prove himself, I wanted to see him kick some serious Death Eater butt. And I got virtually none of what I wanted.

I guess I didn't realize Neville had *already* fulfilled his promise in *Order of the Phoenix*. He's changed so radically from the wuss we met at the beginning of the saga, but somehow I didn't recognize what I was seeing when I saw it.

I do think we'll see more of Neville. But as for proving himself -- I have to admit, he's already done it.

One question hovering over Neville throughout the books is, of course, why did the Sorting Hat put him in Gryffindor (after taking quite a long time to decide) [SS-7]? We only get the barest of hints that he might actually belong there in *Sorcerer's Stone*, when Neville stands up to Harry, Ron and Hermione as they venture forth in quest of the Sorcerer's Stone [SS-16], and is honored for this by

Dumbledore [SS-17].

But after this one moment, it takes several years for Neville to show his stuff again. Finally, in *Order of the Phoenix*, he takes a big step toward courage. He joins the DA [OP-18]. He joins the fight at the Ministry of Magic, even though Harry wants to leave him behind [OP-34]. And he acquits himself well there, even though both his nose and his father's wand are broken [OP-35].

Drumming home the fact that Neville has *already* proven himself as a Gryffindor, McGonagall comes right out and says so, pretty directly:

> *"It's high time your grandmother learned to be proud of the grandson she's got, rather than the one she thinks she ought to have -- particularly after what happened at the Ministry."*
> [HBP-9]

Remember: Neville did all that with the wrong wand. And we know a wizard can't get good results with another wizard's wand [SS-5].

We see more evidence of Neville's incipient courage in *Half-Blood Prince*. He longs for the DA to start up again [HBP-7]. In fact, he's one of only two people to keep the enchanted coin from the DA in his pocket, just in case [HBP-30]. And he again acquits himself well in the Battle for Hogwarts [HBP-28].

All Neville's major set-ups have been paid off. So we don't *need* to see much of him in Book 7, we don't *need* to play out any story lines involving him...

I just sort of hope we do, anyway.

PERCY WEASLEY

If the question about Neville is 'Why did the Hat put him in Gryffindor?' the question regarding Percy has to be: 'Why *didn't* the Hat put him in Slytherin?'

From the moment we meet Percy, we learn he has the kind of ambition that generally drives Slytherins. Right up front, Ron tells us Percy wants to be Minister of Magic someday [CS-4]. Percy is pompous about being a prefect [CS-3] and he has his sights set on being Head Boy from the beginning, enough to be worried that Ron will somehow hurt his chances [CS-9]. (Shouldn't he be worried about the *twins* hurting his chances? Just asking.)

Percy's ambition takes a step forward in each book. He becomes Crouch's personal assistant as a first step [GF-23], then quickly moves up to become Junior Assistant to the Minister of Magic [OP-4]. Given the stifling bureaucracy and political games we've glimpsed at the Ministry of Magic, Percy sure is working the system to move up so fast.

One would think his family would be proud, but no. Ron has his finger on Percy pretty well. Not only does he peg Percy's ultimate ambition right away, but he states his assumption that Percy would do anything -- even commit murder -- to get a promotion [GF-24]. Yeah, it's a joke, but one of those jokes that's uncomfortable because it's a little too close to the truth. Ron also thinks Percy would throw his family to the dementors to advance his own career [GF-27]... and again, he's hitting too close to the truth.

In *Order of the Phoenix,* Percy starts down the road Ron has mapped out for him when he turns his back on his family, calling them "traitors" [OP-4] and accusing them of hanging with "petty criminals" [OP-14]. He also turns his back on Harry when it is politically expedient to do so [OP-14]. He has clearly chosen where his loyalties lie: the Ministry of Magic. Arthur Weasley even thinks Percy has been assigned the task of spying on his own family [OP-4]. To top it all off, Percy shows how corrupt he has become when he describes Dolores Umbridge as "delightful" [OP-14].

Nothing changes in *Half-Blood Prince*. Percy is still hanging in the corridors of power, still a flunky to the powerful, as we see when Rufus Scrimgeour forces him to visit the Weasleys for a "Frosty Christmas." Note that Percy doesn't even have the integrity to refuse to visit the "traitors," but bends to the wishes of whoever can get him his next promotion.

I don't think Percy's story is over. All this power-grubbing has to have a payoff. Could we see Percy actually *become* Minister of Magic? (People have asked J.K. Rowling if *Arthur* Weasley would become Minister, but to the best of my knowledge, no one has asked this about the more likely candidate of Percy.) It'd take a lot of wiping out of senior levels at the Ministry, but Voldemort is certainly capable of that.

I admit, that's a stretch, if only because of Percy's relative youth. But certainly Percy will get yet another promotion in Book 7. And I wouldn't be surprised if some of Ron's prophecies come true: I wouldn't be surprised at all if the set-ups that Percy would harm (or kill?) his family for his own advancement have a payoff.

I also anticipate that Percy could be killed in Book 7. No specific set-ups here... just thinking about people getting what they deserve...

CHAPTER 20

A FEW MORE WIZARDS

Let's look at a few more Wizards of interest, and the payoffs we might expect from them:

RUBEUS HAGRID

To be honest, I don't fully understand the incredible amount of time we have spent with Hagrid, with remarkably little plot payoff (Buckbeak, a lot of set-up for Grawp to scare away the centaurs... and, um, that's about it).

It'd be easy to set him to one side as essentially a lovable character, even comic relief -- but we've spent too much time with him for that. Which means that he must end up being quite important in Book 7.

Let's start by taking a brief detour into the world of alchemy. You'll find fuller discussions in John Granger's book *Looking for God in Harry Potter*, but permit me to dabble in an area about which I know very little.

In the alchemical interpretation of the books, we see a progression from the "black" stage of alchemy (with Sirius *Black* as the representative of this phase) to the "white" stage (with Albus Dumbledore in the forefront here -- note that the name "Albus" comes from the Latin word for *white*). The final stage in the alchemical progression is the "red" stage.

While some have speculated that the "red" stage will find its culmination in a storyline involving the Weasleys, with their red hair, I must disagree. *If* J.K. Rowling is indeed following an alchemical pattern in the books, the stages seem to be marked by the characters' names. So Rubeus Hagrid (whose name "Rubeus" comes from the Latin word for *red*) becomes the focal character for this stage.

If you want more on an alchemical interpretation of the books, I'm the wrong person to ask. Go read what Granger has to say -- and in the meantime, just know this interpretation assures us that Hagrid *will* be important in Book 7.

Okay, back to more traditional set-ups and payoffs.

Practically the very first thing we learn about Hagrid, even before we meet him, is that Dumbledore would trust Hagrid with his life [SS-1]. Indeed, though we've never seen Dumbledore do so, he has certainly entrusted Hagrid with some incredibly important tasks, including the transportation of the Sorcerer's Stone [SS-5], and of Harry himself several times. Dumbledore entrusted the infant Harry with Hagrid (on a flying motorcycle, no less!) [SS-1], entrusted him to pick up Harry and bring him to Hogwarts [SS-4], and, when danger was much higher, entrusted him to escort Harry safely through Diagon Alley in place of the Aurors the Ministry of Magic would have chosen for the task [HBP-6].

But why? We never learn why Dumbledore trusts Hagrid so very deeply (especially given how bad Hagrid is at keeping his mouth shut). Is it because of his impermeability to spells [OP-31, HBP-28]? Is it because of something in Hagrid's past? We just don't know.

One has to wonder what Hagrid's life would have been like

without Dumbledore. We know Hagrid was expelled from Hogwarts after the Chamber of Secrets incident, was banned from doing magic and had his wand snapped [SS-4]. Dumbledore found a place for him at Hogwarts, and has been his staunch supporter and defender ever since. There are plenty of reasons for Hagrid to trust and love Dumbledore. But not much to show us why that trust goes both ways.

So what will happen with Hagrid in Book 7? We haven't been given much to go on. The alchemical reading doesn't guarantee that Hagrid has to die. (Sirius and Dumbledore had to die in order for the story to progress to the next stage, but the red stage has no end, so a death isn't necessary to conclude it.)

But Hagrid may be doomed in Book 7 nonetheless. All Hagrid has done for six books has been show his faithfulness -- and what more faithful act can he serve than to die for those he loves?

Will he die due to a mistake he makes by talking too much? Maybe. That wouldn't be a kind way for him to go, however, and Rowling truly loves this character, probably too much to let him go out in ignominy.

Another possibility: Will he inadvertently betray someone he loves, then die trying to correct his mistake? I think this is a stronger possibility, given that it allows him to demonstrate his faithfulness.

And he may not die: Rowling recently stated that a character she expected to die in Book 7 is getting an *un*expected reprieve. While that character could be virtually anyone, her love for Hagrid certainly puts him high on the list of probabilities.

But where Hagrid is concerned, we can only guess. We don't have specific set-ups for him, despite the huge amount of time we've spent with him. In fact, the biggest set-up we *have* for Hagrid *is* the amount of time we have spent with him. For that reason alone, he must play an important, even a pivotal, role in Book 7.

LUDO BAGMAN

Ludo Bagman is floating out there in the Wizarding World just *waiting* for some Death Eater to exploit him.

We saw how lax he was about security at the Quidditch World Cup [GF-7]. We've seen his rather extreme gambling problem, even extending to wanting to help Harry cheat at the Triwizard Tournament all so he (Ludo) could win a bet [GF-24].

He's also skirted serious trouble in the past. When accused of passing information to Death Eaters [GF-30], he didn't deny it, but merely claimed ignorance of the Death Eaters' involvement with Voldemort, and traded on his fame as a Quidditch player.

This is a man who is extremely susceptible to blackmail. If he knows any useful information at all, he's very likely to spill it to the next person to come along.

We can say he's just weak, feel sorry for him, make excuses (as the Wizengamot clearly did). But look where he is now: On the run after the goblins refused to honor his shady bet on Harry [GF-37] . On the run, just like our other notable weak character, Slughorn, was at the beginning of *Half-Blood Prince*.

Weak? Sure. But Ludo's weakness is the type that gets people killed. Winky was right when she called Ludo a "bad wizard" [GF-382].

Will we see him again in Book 7? We certainly don't have to -- he can stay on the run until Voldemort is really truly dead. But if we need a character to pass information along to the Dark Lord, he's certainly handy... and nicely set-up for the job.

VIKTOR KRUM

Viktor Krum was a fascinating character to have around in *Goblet of Fire* to add some juice to the beginning of the Ron/Hermione relationship. And of course his legendary Quidditch playing was a lot of fun [GF-8] . But I think he may be worth more than that in terms of the plot.

The interesting things about Viktor have to do with his school, Durmstrang. We learn early on that they actually *teach* the Dark Arts there [GF-11]. One would expect a bunch of Slytherins, stuck-up with pride. But Viktor, we learn, prefers Hogwarts to Durmstrang [GF-24]. I think he is the primary one Dumbledore was speaking to when he offered all the foreign students a permanent welcome to Hogwarts after Voldemort returned [GF-37].

And then there's Hermione. She thinks he's nice [GF-24]. Can we really imagine Hermione going out with someone who was really evil? She's smart enough to have Cormac McLaggen's number in *Half-Blood Prince*. And yet she has continued a substantial epistolary relationship with Viktor. Why?

I think it's because we'll see him again in Book 7, bringing his Dark Arts skills to the fight -- and providing a little juice to Ron's jealousy as a bonus.

CHAPTER 21

AND YET MORE WIZARDS

MUNDUNGUS FLETCHER

Mundungus, funny though he may be, is a pretty scummy character. Although he's a member of the Order of the Phoenix, he's a petty thief [OP-5], and he plies his trade pretty diligently throughout the books. So diligently, in fact, that he can't even be trusted to stand guard reliably [OP-1].

Mundungus is personally loyal to Dumbledore, who rescued him once [OP-5]. That loyalty, however, doesn't seem to extend to anyone Dumbledore cares about, given that Mundungus's devotion to his trade takes him back to 12, Grimmauld Place to steal items Harry has inherited after Sirius's death [HBP-12].

Somehow Dumbledore stops Mundungus from doing so [HBP-13], and Mundungus goes into hiding. Not very well, apparently, or maybe the lure of thievery was just too strong for him, as he's now in Azkaban for impersonating an Inferius during a burglary [HBP-21].

It's a good thing we know where Dung is, because Harry might need to have a chat with him in Book 7. At some point, Harry will remember the locket he saw during the scouring of 12, Grimmauld Place, and he'll remember that Sirius's brother was named Regulus, and he'll put the two together and wonder if that very locket mightn't be the locket Horcrux "R.A.B" stole from the Cave.

What if he goes back to 12, Grimmauld Place and finds the locket missing? Well, first he should check Kreacher's stash. But if it's not there, I'd say Mundungus is the next stop in the search for the locket.

And one more set-up about Mundungus, who's already someone we really wouldn't want to trust with our lives. We know he joined the Order out of loyalty to Dumbledore. But where do his loyalties lie now that Dumbledore is dead?

Given all the secrets of the Order that he must know, maybe it's a *really* good thing that he's in Azkaban.

RUFUS SCRIMGEOUR

We first met Scrimgeour in *Half-Blood Prince* [HBP-1]. But we were actually introduced to him indirectly back in *Order of the Phoenix*, and it wasn't an introduction that should make us feel comfortable with him. We learn, in a throwaway line, that Scrimgeour is suspicious of the Aurors who are members of the Order [OP-7].

That suspicious nature continues once Scrimgeour comes into power. We see early on that he and Dumbledore are in disagreement [HBP-4]. Every time we see him from that point on, Scrimgeour overtly sets himself against Dumbledore.

We know that Scrimgeour, cynical manipulator that he is, wants Harry to serve as a public relations shill for the Ministry. He also wants information he can't get otherwise, specifically about Dumbledore [HBP-16]. (Just think how many avenues he must have tried before dragging Percy to the Weasleys so he could corner Harry!)

And we know Harry's got his number:

> *"...You never get it right, you people, do you? Either we've got Fudge, pretending everything's lovely while people get murdered right under his nose, or we've got you, chucking the wrong people into jail and trying to pretend you've got 'the Chosen One' working for you!"*
>
> *"So you're not 'the Chosen One'?" said Scrimgeour.*
>
> *"I thought you said it didn't matter either way?" said Harry, with a bitter laugh. "Not to you anyway."*
>
> *"I shouldn't have said that," said Scrimgeour quickly. "It was tactless--"*
>
> *"No, it was honest," said Harry. "One of the only honest things you've said to me. You don't care whether I live or die, but you do care that I help you convince everyone you're winning the war against Voldemort..." [HBP-16]*

What will we see from Rufus Scrimgeour in Book 7? More of the same, I expect. He has clearly drawn battle lines between himself and Dumbledore, just as strong, perhaps, as the lines drawn against Voldemort. And as Harry has made it quite clear that he is "Dumbledore's man through and through" [HBP-16, 30], undoubtedly Scrimgeour will continue the adversarial relationship against Harry.

However, with all the story lines to be fulfilled in Book 7, I have to think that any obstacles the Ministry of Magic throws up against Harry's quest will be minor compared to the quest itself.

OLLIVANDER AND FLOREAN FORTESCUE

Ollivander and Fortescue disappeared at the same time [HBP-6]. But there was a big difference between them: Fortescue, based on the evidence of his shop, was clearly dragged off kicking and screaming. Ollivander, on the other hand, left his shop in good shape, with no signs of any struggle. So we must ask: Did he leave with the Death Eaters voluntarily?

Whether he did or not, as Mr. Weasley points out, it's not good for Voldemort's side to have Ollivander in their clutches. As the best wandmaker around, he could be uniquely valuable to them.

I expect we will see Fortescue again, probably at the end of Book 7, as part of the celebration of Voldemort's defeat. As for Ollivander... Well, I think we'll see him again too. But on whose side?

A FEW THOUGHTS ON WIZARD QUALIFICATION

We know coming of age and being "qualified" as a wizard are two different things. It seems one becomes qualified upon taking one's N.E.W.T.s. Hagrid is certainly "of age" but, having been expelled from Hogwarts, never became "fully-qualified." The Weasley twins, having dropped out of Hogwarts, presumably are also unqualified, despite their extreme skill as wizards.

So Harry, who has announced *his* intention to drop out of Hogwarts, will also presumably not be a "fully-qualified" wizard. Which makes the following statement by Dumbledore at the Cave of interest:

> *"Voldemort will not have cared about the weight, but about*
> *the amount of magical power that crossed his lake. I rather think*

an enchantment will have been placed upon this boat so that only one wizard at a time will be able to sail in it."

"But then--?"

"I do not think you will count, Harry: You are underage and unqualified. Voldemort would never have expected a sixteen-year-old to reach this place: I think it unlikely that your powers will register compared to mine." [HBP-26]

So Harry slips through under Voldemort's radar, as it were, because he is underage and unqualified. Now he will be of age, of course, when (or shortly after) the final book begins. But will it make a difference that he is unqualified? Will that somehow help him to avoid any of Voldemort's traps?

One can only hope...

CHAPTER 22

SEVERUS AND HARRY

The most fascinating character in the whole *Harry Potter* canon is definitely Severus Snape.

Snape hates Harry. That much is very clear even from their first encounter in Potions class, when Snape makes Harry look stupid and mocks him in front of everyone: "Our new -- *celebrity*" (a moment which is even better in the movie! -- thank you, Alan Rickman!) [SS-8]. Harry draws the logical conclusion:

> *Harry told Hagrid about Snape's lesson. Hagrid, like Ron, told Harry not to worry about it, that Snape liked hardly any of the students.*
>
> *"But he seemed to really hate me."*
>
> *"Rubbish!" said Hagrid. "Why should he?"*
>
> *Yet Harry couldn't help thinking that Hagrid didn't quite meet his eyes when he said that.* [SS-8]

Harry's suspicions about Snape's feelings toward him are confirmed by Quirrell:

> *"But Snape always seemed to hate me so much."*

"Oh, he does," said Quirrell casually, "heavens, yes. He was at Hogwarts with your father, didn't you know? They loathed each other. But he never wanted you __dead__." [SS-17]

Yes, Snape hates Harry. It's established early on in the series, and we could print citation after citation of confirming behavior on Snape's part.

But while Snape may talk the talk of hatred, he doesn't always walk the walk. In fact, he goes out of his way repeatedly to *protect* Harry. Let's take a look at how.

In the most obvious example (and one of J.K. Rowling's prime examples of narrative misdirection), Snape saves Harry's life during the Quidditch match in *Sorcerer's Stone*, muttering the countercurse against Quirrell's curse. Quirrell confirms that he himself was trying to kill Harry [SS-17], and that in fact, Snape was suspicious of him throughout the story, and pursued him even as he (Quirrell) was, under the influence of Lord Voldemort, pursuing Harry [SS-17].

Snape's next major attempt to protect Harry comes in *Prisoner of Azkaban*. Harry actually doesn't need protection from Sirius Black, but no one knows this. Snape is aware of the overall efforts to protect Harry, and seems to be part of them [PA-14]. Snape even insists that, in following Harry and friends to the Shrieking Shack, he not only protected Harry from possible death at the hands of Sirius, but also from possible attack from werewolf Lupin [PA-19]. Again, *we* know Harry was safe, and we can see ulterior motives in Snape's actions -- but from Snape's point of view, it's certainly a quite credible claim that he put himself at risk to follow and protect Harry.

Moving on to *Goblet of Fire*: Snape searches the fake Moody's office. Hermione links this to Snape's looking after Harry [GF-26]. Hermione actually mentions several times that Snape saved Harry's life in their first year [GF-27]. Why, we have to ask, does she keep bringing this up? Is she serving as the voice of the author, reminding us of something *we* need to remember... or is it another case of narrative misdirection?

In *Order of the Phoenix*, Snape takes several explicit steps to protect Harry (and the Order itself). When Umbridge goes after Harry, Snape provides fake Veritaserum [OP-37], not only keeping Harry from spilling secrets that should not be spilled, but also protecting Harry from further punishment by the sadistic Umbridge. When Harry spits out a coded message while being held captive in Umbridge's office, Snape, though pretending he doesn't know what Harry means, instead takes him seriously, warning the Order and setting in motion the steps that indeed save Harry's life (not to mention the lives of Hermione, Ron, Luna, Neville, and Ginny) [OP-37].

Finally, in *Half-Blood Prince*, even as Harry is justifiably filled with hatred for Snape, who has just (apparently) killed Dumbledore, Snape continues to protect Harry. He repeatedly keeps him from performing the Cruciatus Curse [HBP-28], the Unforgivable Curse that Harry seems to find the most tempting. He also gives Harry a very sensible warning that, were Harry to heed it (unlikely, given the person speaking and the circumstances), would save Harry a lot of trouble:

> *"Blocked again and again and again until you learn to keep your mouth shut and your mind closed, Potter!" sneered Snape, deflecting the curse once more.* [HBP-28]

There's one more thing Snape does here... Or actually something he *doesn't* do. With Harry in his hands, at his mercy, Snape does *not* take him to Lord Voldemort.

This negative set-up, as it were, is a clue of the highest order. We must ask ourselves: If Snape is really in the service of the Dark

Lord, why would he not deliver Harry Potter to him? Oh yeah, he has an excuse, which he gives to the other Death Eaters on the scene who indeed want to take Harry to Voldemort:

> *"Have you forgotten our orders? Potter belongs to the Dark Lord -- we are to leave him!"* [HBP-28]

Well, maybe in the heat of the moment the Death Eaters buy this, but to those of us who remember set-ups from previous books, it's totally bogus!

Have we forgotten how badly fake Moody wanted to deliver to Voldemort the one thing the Dark Lord wanted above all else: Harry:

> *Moody's face was suddenly lit with an insane smile. "Tell me he told them that I, I alone remained faithful... prepared to risk everything to deliver to him the one thing he wanted above all... you."* [GF-35]

Fake Moody clearly knows the value of Harry to Voldemort, and makes it clear the Dark Lord would *not* object to having a servant do the dirty work of capturing Harry:

> *"The Dark Lord didn't manage to kill you, Potter, and he so wanted to," whispered Moody. "Imagine how he will reward me when he finds I have done it for him. I gave you to him -- the thing he needed above all to regenerate -- and then I killed you for him. I will be honored beyond all other Death Eaters. I will be his dearest, his closest supporter... closer than a son...."* [GF-35]

Note also that through the entire battle at the Ministry of Magic in *Order of the Phoenix*, the working assumption of the Death Eaters is that turning Harry over to Voldemort is a *good* thing.

So why in the world does Snape *fail* to do the one thing which would indeed, if he is truly 'Voldemort's man through and through,' give him power, reward, honor and fame? Why does he *fail* to deliver Harry to Voldemort when such failure could, arguably, lead to Voldemort's wrath and even Snape's death at Voldemort's hands?

One (weak) answer could lie in the concept of the life-debt. We all know about Peter Pettigrew's life-debt to Harry, discussed in Chapter 8. But could Snape also have a life-debt to James, which is now only payable through Harry? Dumbledore seems to imply so at the end of *Sorcerer's Stone*:

> *"...And then, your father did something Snape could never forgive."*

> *"What?"*

> *"He saved his life."*

> "What?"

> *"Yes..." said Dumbledore dreamily. "Funny, the way people's minds work, isn't it? Professor Snape couldn't bear being in your father's debt.... I do believe he worked so hard to protect you this year because he felt that would make him and your father even. Then he could go back to hating your father's memory in peace...."* [SS-17]

When James saved Snape's life, it may have created a life-debt between them, as Harry's saving Pettigrew's life created a life-debt acknowledged by Dumbledore. Could this be the reason (or *a* reason) why Snape is so consistently protective of Harry, despite his obvious hatred of him?

Or does Snape protect Harry, not turn Harry over to

Voldemort because he is in fact working secretly *against* Voldemort? We are explicitly led to believe this in *Order of the Phoenix,* even though it does seem rather contradicted by Snape's killing of Dumbledore. We'll come back to a discussion of Snape's loyalties in Chapter 23, but for now, let's just admire the complexity of the set-ups we've been given.

Snape hates Harry. True. Snape protects Harry. Also true. The contradiction between these facts is, I would say, the great tension pulling at the fabric of the entire *Harry Potter* story.

Oh, and how does Harry feel about Snape, we should ask. Well, duh. Harry hates Snape. And after Snape's putative murder of Dumbledore, Harry hates Snape with a depth of hatred unseen previously in the books.

And yet... And yet...

Harry deeply appreciated the Half-Blood Prince, valued him, saw him as a sort of mentor. Will Harry shove those feelings and thoughts to the back of his mind? Or will he explore them, try to reconcile this contradiction between his feelings (hatred of Snape) and his actions (appreciation and use of the Prince's hints and help)?

In addition, Harry has the potential to truly understand Snape. We see this not only in his "relationship" to the Half-Blood Prince, but in his flash of pity toward the teenage Snape he saw when he dived into "Snape's Worse Memory" during their Occlumency lessons [OP-28].

Snape is on the run. Harry is not likely to run into him for some time, one would think, in Book 7. But he does have access to Snape, if he chooses to take advantage of it. That potions book is still sitting there in the Room of Requirement [HBP-24]. Maybe Harry will want it for its obvious spell-casting value. Or maybe he will find it more valuable for what it might tell him about his nemesis and rescuer, Severus Snape.

It's all been set-up, for us and for Harry. All he has to do is fetch the book and see what secrets it reveals.

CHAPTER 23

SNAPE: LEGILIMENCY AND LOYALTY

LEGILIMENCY.

Snape's command of Legilimency and Occlumency is set up from the very beginning of the *Harry Potter* saga, initially without our realizing what the set-ups are pointing to.

Harry has the feeling that Snape can read minds during the search for the Sorcerer's Stone [SS-13]. He has the same feeling when Snape is the one to greet him and Ron after they fly the Ford Anglia to Hogwarts [CS-5]. Again when Snape questions him about Draco having seen Harry's head in Hogsmeade [PA-14]. Yet again when Harry arrives at Hogwarts covered in blood after Draco beats him up on the train [HBP-8].

Snape uses Legilimency legitimately and openly, of course, during his ill-fated Occlumency lessons with Harry, in which he has pretty free access to Harry's mind, including to images Harry might choose to block, such as the more embarrassing moments with the Dursleys, and the image of Rookwood before Voldemort [OP-26].

We also see Snape use Legilimency overtly as a weapon when Harry lies to him about the Sectumsempra spell [HBP-24]. In this instance, Snape's use of Legilimency has a flavor of the Imperius Curse to it. Harry *knows* what Snape is about to do, *wants* to keep Snape out of his mind, but simply lacks the skills to do so. This is also the only time (other than in Occlumency lessons) when Harry is explicitly aware of Snape's presence in his mind.

It's a good reminder for us (and Harry) of just how much Harry *needs* to learn the one thing which Snape, in admittedly hostile circumstances, warned him he needed: To *close his mind* [HBP-28]!

Dumbledore tells us the key element of Legilimency is the ability to know when one is being lied to [OP-37]. Snape of course uses this skill to know that Harry is lying to him about the Potions book [HBP-24]. But Snape needs this skill, and its corresponding skill of Occlumency, much more in his dealings with Voldemort.

As soon as we learn what Occlumency is, we learn Snape is a "superb Occlumens" [OP-24]. He must be, since his Occlumency skills apparently allow him to get away with lying to Voldemort. Not only does he get away with it, he flaunts it:

> *"...Do you really think that the Dark Lord has not asked me each and every one of those questions? And do you really think that, had I not been able to give satisfactory answers, I would be sitting here talking to you?"*
>
> *[Bellatrix] hesitated.*
>
> *"I know he believes you, but..."*
>
> *"You think he is mistaken? Or that I have somehow hoodwinked him? Fooled the Dark Lord, the greatest wizard, the most accomplished Legilimens the world has ever seen?"* [HBP-2]

But that's *exactly* what Snape appears to have done... which, in my book, makes *Snape* the most accomplished Occlumens the world has ever seen.

However, it's important to note: Snape couldn't block Harry's fledgling attempts at Legilimency [OP-26] during the episode in which Harry sees the images of Snape as an abused child. This set-up points out that Snape's Legilimency isn't flawless. What would happen to the Order of the Phoenix if the wall of his Occlumency were to be breached by Voldemort?

Another payoff we might see from Snape's talents in Legilimency and Occlumency could occur in further confrontations between Snape and Harry. Note that in the Battle at Hogwarts, Snape was able to block Harry's every curse, every spell, *before* Harry could cast it. Snape even blocks Harry's *nonverbal* attempt to cast Levicorpus, making it clear that he is using Legilimency to do so [HBP-28].

If Snape can do this, then Harry can't fight him. Or at least, he can't fight him and win. Snape will best Harry every time... until Harry learns to *close his mind...*

Occlumency is, of course, key to the mystery of Snape's loyalties, as Lupin makes clear by assuming Snape kept the Order of the Phoenix from knowing his true loyalties through Occlumency [HBP-29]. (Note that this raises the probability that several, even most, of the Order are also Legilimens.)

SNAPE'S LOYALTIES

It's common knowledge that Snape is a *former* Death Eater, as Dumbledore testifies for the record:

> *"No!"* shouted Karkaroff, *straining at the chains that bound him to the chair. "I assure you! Severus Snape is a Death Eater!"*

> *Dumbledore had gotten to his feet.*

"I have given evidence already on this matter," he said calmly. *"Severus Snape was indeed a Death Eater. However, he rejoined our side before Lord Voldemort's downfall and turned spy for us, at great personal risk. He is now no more a Death Eater than I am."* [GF-30].

It's important that the Wizengamot's clearing Snape's name is based on *Dumbledore's* testimony, not on Snape's. Throughout the series, Dumbledore's reiterated trust in Snape stands as the primary reason anyone else is willing to trust Snape at all.

Dumbledore's trust in Snape is so well-known that even the Death Eaters, despite their natural suspicions, know of it and have no argument against it. Snape's position appears to be unassailable:

"And through all this we are supposed to believe Dumbledore has never suspected you?" asked Bellatrix. *"He has no idea of your true allegiance, he trusts you implicitly still?"*

"I have played my part well," said Snape. *"And you overlook Dumbledore's greatest weakness: He has to believe the best of people. I spun him a tale of deepest remorse when I joined his staff, fresh from my Death Eater days, and he embraced me with open arms.... through all these years, he has never stopped trusting Severus Snape, and therein lies my great value to the Dark Lord."*

Bellatrix still looked unhappy, though she appeared unsure how best to attack Snape next..." [HBP-2]

But why? *Why* does (or did) Dumbledore trust Snape?

We simply don't know. Or we don't know much. A few people might know more: Barty Crouch, Jr. for one (here in disguise as Fake-Moody):

"'Course Dumbledore trusts you," growled Moody. "He's a trusting man, isn't he? Believes in second chances. But me -- I say there are spots that don't come off, Snape. Spots that never come off, d'you know what I mean?" [GF-25]

Unfortunately Barty, his soul neatly sucked out by the dementors, isn't around to tell us what those "second chances" might have involved.

But no one else really seems to know much of the details. It's up to Harry to spill what little Dumbledore has told him to others of the Order:

"[Dumbledore] always hinted that he had an ironclad reason for trusting Snape," muttered Professor McGonagall, now dabbing at the corners of her leaking eyes with a tartan-edged handkerchief. "I mean... with Snape's history... of course people were bound to wonder... but Dumbledore told me explicitly that Snape's repentance was absolutely genuine.... Wouldn't hear a word against him!"

"I'd love to know what Snape told him to convince him," said Tonks.

"I know," said Harry, and they all turned to look at him. "Snape passed Voldemort the information that made Voldemort hunt down my mum and dad. Then Snape told Dumbledore he hadn't realized what he was doing, he was really sorry he'd done it, sorry that they were dead."

They all stared at him.

"And Dumbledore believed that?" said Lupin incredulously. "Dumbledore believed Snape was sorry James was dead? Snape hated James...." [HBP-29]

This is one of the key exchanges that make my dramatic senses quiver. The set-up, I believe, may be in what *isn't* said.

Lupin is absolutely right: Snape wouldn't be sorry that *James* was dead. Given the depth of the hatred we've seen Snape express for James, I can't believe Snape would feel any need to repent of any action that would lead to James's death. Lupin's quite correct to be incredulous about it.

But James isn't the only one who died that night. Lily died, too. So if James's death can't be what drove Snape to switch loyalties, at the potential cost of his own life, could it be Lily's death that caused him to do so?

Add to this the fact that Snape *never* mentioned Lily to Harry. *Never.* And Lily was, we learn from Slughorn, a great Potions student. A perfect set-up for Snape to taunt Harry a little more: "Your mother could have handled this Potion with her eyes closed. Clearly the apple fell far from the tree."

Given this information, Snape *should* have mentioned Lily, at least in passing. We shouldn't have had to wait till *Half-Blood Prince* to learn Lily was a "dab hand" at Potions.

Could it be Snape *couldn't* mention Lily -- couldn't mention her because he had had feelings for her -- feelings so strong as to give him the courage to switch to the side of good and become a clandestine warrior against the side of evil?

Again, we have no real set-ups for this theory (which has certainly been proposed elsewhere). But here it's the fact that we have *no* information of any kind, when we should, that makes me wonder.

The real question of course is: Why *doesn't* Dumbledore tell

Harry the whole story about Snape's repentance? Harry asks point blank just before Voldemort returns to his body:

> "What made you think he'd really stopped supporting Voldemort, Professor?"

> Dumbledore held Harry's gaze for a few seconds, and then said, "That, Harry is a matter between Professor Snape and myself." [GF-30]

Perhaps it's understandable why Dumbledore doesn't spill the beans at this point in the story. Voldemort has not yet returned. The overall battle is not yet at a crisis stage, and there may be no need for Harry to know the answer. Snape's repentance is a thing of the past, not as relevant as it will shortly become.

But after Harry learns it was Snape who told Voldemort about the prophecy, after he knows the very information Dumbledore has striven to keep from him all these years, Dumbledore *still* refuses to tell Harry information which Harry could easily insist he has the right to know:

> "You have no idea of the remorse Professor Snape felt when he realized how Lord Voldemort had interpreted the prophecy, Harry. I believe it to be the greatest regret of his life and the reason that he returned --"

> "But he's a very good Occlumens, isn't he, sir?" said Harry, whose voice was shaking with the effort of keeping it steady. "And isn't Voldemort convinced that Snape's on his side, even now? Professor... how can you be sure Snape's on our side?"

> Dumbledore did not speak for a moment; he looked as though he was trying to make up his mind about something. At

last he said, "I am sure. I trust Severus Snape completely."
[HBP-25]

What was Dumbledore trying to make up his mind about there? Was he toying with the idea that maybe he *shouldn't* have trusted Snape so implicitly? Was he momentarily tempted to abandon that trust? Or was he considering whether to tell Harry what he knew?

Given the absolute nature of Dumbledore's trust in Snape throughout, given that Harry provides him with no new knowledge, I believe it is the latter. Which raises another question: Who was Dumbledore trying to protect by not telling Harry what he knew? Harry? Or Snape? (Or both?)

Without Dumbledore's explicit statement giving reasons for his trust in Snape, how could Harry possibly learn the truth of Snape's loyalties in Book 7? Well (positing that Snape is still Dumbledore's man), I have already suggested one avenue: If Fawkes should align himself with Snape, Harry had better pay attention to what this might mean!

Harry could figure it out on his own, however. We have the subtlest of set-ups when we compare Harry's and Snape's emotional reactions when put into similar, equally horrific circumstances.

One of the worst moments of Harry's eventful life so far has to be when, in the Cave, he must force-feed Dumbledore the green potion despite Dumbledore's pleas for him to stop, and despite the strong possibility that the potion could be deadly:

> **Hating** *himself,* **repulsed** *by what he was doing, Harry forced the goblet back toward Dumbledore's mouth and tipped it, so that Dumbledore drank the remainder of the potion inside.* [HBP-26, emphasis added]

Compare this to Snape's emotional reaction at the moment he is about to kill Dumbledore:

> *Snape gazed for a moment at Dumbledore, and there was* **revulsion** *and* **hatred** *etched in the harsh lines of his face.*
> [HBP-27, emphasis added]

Harry hates himself in the passage above. Snape, we're not so sure about. Does he hate himself? Or Dumbledore?

But notice the words used to describe their reactions. "Hatred." "Revulsion" ("repulse" is essentially the verb form of "revulsion"). To be repulsed, to feel revulsion, is literally to push away from something. Harry is pushing away from the task he has to perform, that of poisoning Dumbledore, of feeding him the last of the green potion, possibly the killing dose.

What is Snape repulsed by? Not Dumbledore. That wouldn't make sense, when Dumbledore has shown him extreme mercy over the years, has trusted him when no one else would. No, I think that, just like Harry, Snape feels revulsion for the task he must do.

I doubt these two will get a chance to sit down and compare notes. But if they did, wouldn't it be interesting to find all they have in common.

Without that conversation, however, or its equivalent, why Dumbledore trusted Snape remains the prime unanswered question of the whole series. I trust that J.K. Rowling will not leave this thread hanging in Book 7!

CHAPTER 24

"STOPPERED DEATH"

If the most important unanswered question in *Harry Potter* is: Why did Dumbledore trust Snape?, the follow-up question is almost equally important: Was Dumbledore wrong to trust Snape?

On the surface, the answer to this question is apparently yes, as everyone in the Order of the Phoenix clearly feels at the end of *Half-Blood Prince*.

However, if one accepts, or even wants to consider, the incredibly elegant theory of "Stoppered Death" originally proposed by Cathy Liesner of The Leaky Cauldron (www.the-leaky-cauldron.org), then everything apparent turns on its head.

(I am loath to publish someone else's theory here. However Liesner, who originally posted this theory in an online class (hosted by Barnes & Noble and moderated by John Granger and Liesner) in August 2005, has not posted it or published it anywhere else, to the best of my knowledge. That message board has long since been closed and is no longer accessible. I think "Stoppered Death" is such an important theory that I recap it here. Let me make it very clear, however, that all credit for the original theory must go to Liesner, with subsequent elucidations made by class participants in the Barnes & Noble class.)

There are a lot of *Harry Potter* theories out there. So many bend and twist the stories to make them fit the theory, or they rely on obscure references while ignoring other evidence at their leisure. But the Stoppered Death theory does neither. Rather, it answers questions simply and elegantly without contradicting evidence we already have. I am more and more convinced Liesner's theory is right.

The Stoppered Death theory is rooted in Harry's first potions class with Snape.

That first class is referenced explicitly several times in *Half-Blood Prince*. First, when Harry is called upon to brew an antidote for a poison:

> *And there it was, scrawled right across a long list of antidotes:*
>
> *Just shove a bezoar down their throats.*
>
> *Harry stared at those words for a moment. Hadn't he once, long ago, heard of bezoars? Hadn't Snape mentioned them in their first ever Potions lesson? A stone taken from the stomach of a goat, which will protect from most poisons.* [HBP-18]

Hermione also refers to that first Potions class when remonstrating against Harry's use of the Half-Blood Prince's Potions book:

> *"Don't start, Hermione," said Harry. "If it hadn't been for the Prince, Ron wouldn't be sitting here now."*
>
> *"He would be if you'd just listened to Snape in our first year," said Hermione dismissively.* [HBP-19]

When J.K. Rowling sees fit to mention something so many

times (especially when she doesn't have an immediate plot-related reason to do so), we must treat the mention as if a glowing arrow were pointing at it, commanding our attention. So let's go back and see what else Professor Snape may have said to his first-year students:

> *"I can teach you how to bottle fame, brew glory, even stopper death -- if you aren't as big a bunch of dunderheads as I usually have to teach."* [SS-8]

Liesner proposes that Snape has done just what he said he could do: He has "stoppered death" for Dumbledore. Her theory answers a lot of questions without creating the "Yeah, but what about--" responses that are so common with less elegant theories.

In *Half-Blood Prince*, Dumbledore went out to destroy the Ring Horcrux, and by his own words, doing so almost killed him:

> *"Had it not been -- forgive me the lack of seemly modesty -- for my own prodigious skill, and for Professor Snape's timely action when I returned to Hogwarts, desperately injured, I might not have lived to tell the tale..."* [HBP-10]

What did Snape do for Dumbledore upon his return to Hogwarts? Let's say Snape "stoppered" his death: Postponed it, but not indefinitely.

This theory answers the question: What happened to Dumbledore's hand? In every scene in which Dumbledore appears in *Half-Blood Prince*, our attention is pulled to that blackened, burned hand. Why, we must wonder, hasn't Dumbledore fixed it? Well, what if he couldn't? What if he's lucky to have that blackened hand -- because the only other option was death?

We see support for this in the Dark curse that struck Katie

Bell. Dumbledore reports on Katie's prognosis shortly after she receives the curse:

> *"...She appears to have brushed the necklace with the smallest possible amount of skin: There was a tiny hole in her glove. Had she put it on, had she even held it in her ungloved hand, she would have died, perhaps instantly. Luckily Professor Snape was able to do enough to prevent a rapid spread of the curse--"*
>
> *"Why him?" asked Harry quickly. "Why not Madam Pomfrey?"* [HBP-13]

A rapid *spread* of the curse. Hmm. Could that be what happened to Dumbledore? He reached Snape in time for Snape to prevent a rapid spread of the curse laid on the Ring Horcrux, a curse that, as we heard from Dumbledore, would otherwise have killed him.

Harry has a legitimate objection here: Why go to Snape for healing? Why *not* Madam Pomfrey?

Harry's objection is met, however, if we look through *Half-Blood Prince,* where we see that Snape really is the go-to guy for major healing.

Snape heals Dumbledore after the Ring Horcrux. He heals Katie when Madam Pomfrey, according to Dumbledore, would not have been able to do so. He heals Draco when Harry performs the Sectumsempra curse on him -- and knows what Madam Pomfrey needs to do to finish up the healing. He's the one person Dumbledore insists on seeing when he returns from the Cave (because Dumbledore needs Snape to "restopper" his death, perhaps?).

There's more. When Bill is attacked by Fenrir Greyback, even Harry thinks Snape might have cared for him better than Madam Pomfrey, who has no cure available. And think back to *Prisoner of Azkaban*, where Snape keeps werewolf Lupin functional through the full moon by brewing up a potion that hardly anyone, according to Lupin, is able to brew.

Snape the Healer. That's a twist in our thinking, isn't it? But the evidence is there.

So now back to Dumbledore. If we buy the Stoppered Death theory, Dumbledore has been "Dead-Wizard-Walking" since the beginning of *Half-Blood Prince*.

This does more than just explain his burned hand. It explains why, after so many years of withholding information from Harry, he is now so eager to pour information *into* him: Dumbledore knows his time is extremely limited, and is essentially using his tutoring sessions with Harry as his own version of Christ's Upper Room Discourse: He is telling his disciple everything he can to prepare him for the task ahead.

The "Stoppered Death" theory even explains why Dumbledore finally gave Snape the treasured Defense against the Dark Arts job after so many years! Knowing the position had been cursed by Voldemort so that no one remained in it more than one year, Dumbledore, realizing how limited his time was going to be, realizing that Snape would most likely have to unstopper his lurking death and would therefore become a pariah, finally allowed Snape the prize he had desired for so long.

"Stoppered Death" also helps us understand just why Dumbledore trusts Snape so much. Snape holds Dumbledore's life in his hands! (Talk about a life-debt!)

Of course, Dumbledore avowed his trust in Snape long before the Ring Horcrux incident, and we clearly don't have the whole story, as discussed in Chapter 23. But the Stoppered Death theory is consistent with what we *do* know. It makes sense.

The Stoppered Death theory also draws a big flashing arrow to a comment of Dumbledore's on top of the Astronomy Tower just before his death. As he offers to take Draco under the protection of the Order of the Phoenix, he says:

"He cannot kill you if you are already dead..." [HBP-27]

What an odd comment. The rest of Dumbledore's speech to Draco talks of hiding, of protecting... But could it be that Harry will be able to look back on this comment and realize that, no, Snape did *not* kill Dumbledore with the Avada Kedavra on the Lightning-Struck Tower... because Dumbledore was *already dead* at the time?

The Stoppered Death theory, to my mind, makes Snape's actions make sense -- and is fully set-up throughout the books. It answers the question "Was Dumbledore wrong to trust Snape?" with a resounding no.

Now all we need to know is the rest of the answer to the question "*Why* did Dumbledore trust Snape?" Unfortunately, the elegant Stoppered Death theory can't answer *that* question for us.

CHAPTER 25

HORCRUXES

The plot of Book 7 will necessarily center on Harry's destruction of Voldemort's Horcruxes. We have set-ups aplenty, sometimes even outright gimmes handed to us on a silver platter regarding the various Horcruxes... Yet we still don't know enough about how one makes -- or destroys -- a Horcrux to speak very definitively at all.

But let's take a look at what we do know.

First we need to remind ourselves that J.K. Rowling began setting up the Horcruxes at the very beginning of the story. One of the very first things Harry learns about Voldemort is essentially (with hindsight) the fact that he has been removing parts of his soul. As Hagrid points out:

> *"Some say he died. Codswallop, in my opinion. Dunno if he had enough human left in him to die."* [SS-4]

We know Horcruxes are an obscure branch of very dark magic. Dumbledore has banned the very subject from Hogwarts, and there are no books about them in the Hogwarts library [HBP-23]. The subject is so *very* banned that Slughorn even took steps to protect his own memories so no one would know he had so much as discussed the subject with Tom Riddle [HBP-17]. He also lied to

Harry, claiming he knew nothing about the subject [HBP-18].

In the very conversation that Slughorn tried to keep from Harry, we get a basic course in Horcruxes:

> *"A Horcrux is the word used for an object in which a person has concealed part of their soul.... Well, you split your soul, you see," said Slughorn, "and hide part of it in an object outside the body. Then, even if one's body is attacked or destroyed, one cannot die, for part of the soul remains earthbound and undamaged. But of course, existence in such a form.... few would want it, Tom, very few. Death would be preferable."*
>
> *But Riddle's hunger was now apparent; his expression was greedy, he could no longer hide his longing.*
>
> *"How do you split your soul?"*
>
> *"Well," said Slughorn uncomfortably, "you must understand that the soul is supposed to remain intact and whole. Splitting it is an act of violation, it is against nature."*
>
> *"But how do you do it?"*
>
> *"By an act of evil -- the supreme act of evil. By committing murder. Killing rips the soul apart. The wizard intent upon creating a Horcrux would use the damage to his advantage: He would encase the torn portion --"*
>
> *"Encase? But how--?"*
>
> *"There is a spell, do not ask me, I don't know!" said Slughorn...* [HBP-23]

Note, by the way, that while Voldemort may have learned the

basics about Horcruxes from Slughorn, Slughorn did *not* teach him how to create one. Making one wonder... where *did* he learn it?

We also learn in this conversation of Tom Riddle's intent to split his soul into *seven* pieces, seven being the most powerfully magical number. Given that he must leave one of the seven pieces remaining inside his body, that leaves six Horcruxes for Harry to seek and destroy.

It's clear Voldemort created more than one Horcrux by his "remarkably blasé" attitude toward the diary [HBP-23]. He was so very cavalier with an object containing a piece of his own soul, using it to reopen the Chamber of Secrets. This seems to indicate, as Dumbledore points out, that he must have had other Horcruxes already in hand. Voldemort had thus become the first wizard ever to tear his soul in more than two pieces.

This fact, which we learn from Dumbledore, points out a crucial piece of information about Horcrux creation: Murder alone does not automatically create a Horcrux. There are undoubtedly many wizards who have committed more than one murder in their lives. Voldemort himself has certainly committed more murders than those used to create his Horcruxes. Yet only Voldemort has had more than one Horcrux. The soul may "rip" because of the murder, but it's the *use* of that rip that matters.

So Voldemort has created six Horcruxes, with the remaining part of his soul still within his body [HBP-23]. Two of them -- the Diary and the Ring -- have been destroyed, with the Ring's destruction coming at the very great cost of Dumbledore's hand [HBP-23]... or, if we believe the "Stoppered Death" theory, at the even greater cost of Dumbledore's life.

These destructions, however, apparently didn't register with Lord Voldemort:

"Does Voldemort know when a Horcrux is destroyed, sir? Can he feel it?" Harry asked, ignoring the portraits.

"A very interesting question, Harry. I believe not. I believe that Voldemort is now so immersed in evil, and those crucial parts of himself have been detached for so long, he does not feel as we do. Perhaps, at the point of death, he might be aware of his loss... but he was not aware, for instance, that the diary had been destroyed until he forced the truth out of Lucius Malfoy..." [HBP-23]

This fact has an obvious payoff for Book 7 -- and a valuable one for Harry! When Harry destroys the remaining Horcruxes, Voldemort won't know he has done so. Harry can thus work stealthily without tickling the sleeping dragon, as it were, up till the moment he has to confront Voldemort himself. Were Voldemort to be aware of Horcrux destruction, he would undoubtedly drop everything and race to the scene of the crime. However, he isn't aware.

We also know that, without his Horcruxes, Voldemort *will* be mortal:

Harry sat in thought for a moment, then asked, "So if all of his Horcruxes are destroyed, Voldemort could be killed?"

"Yes, I think so," said Dumbledore. *"Without his Horcruxes, Voldemort will be a mortal man with a maimed and diminished soul..."* [HBP-23]

This makes Harry's task for Book 7 quite clear: Destroy the remaining Horcruxes, then destroy the diminished (but still dangerous) Voldemort. Harry even sums it up for us:

"So," said Harry, *"the diary's gone, the ring's gone. The*

cup, the locket, and the snake are still intact, and you think there might be a Horcrux that was once Ravenclaw's or Gryffindor's?"

"An admirably succinct and accurate summary, yes," said Dumbledore, bowing his head. [HBP-23]

That's what we'll turn to next: The actual Horcruxes themselves. The diary. The ring. The locket. The cup. Nagini. And.....??

CHAPTER 26

THE HORCRUXES WE KNOW

Rarely has J.K. Rowling spelled out expository details as clearly as she has regarding (most of) Voldemort's Horcruxes. (Perhaps she realizes she has a lot of story still to tell, and relatively few pages left in which to tell it!)

Let's take a look at the individual Horcruxes, and at the set-ups that accrue to them.

THE DIARY

The Diary is our major "living" example of a Horcrux, the only one we've see in action other than Nagini (as far as we know). As such, it raises some interesting questions.

The Diary, rather than just sitting around like, well, an object, is indeed living and active, bringing forth a "memory" of Tom Riddle which can act as if alive, so much so that this "memory" even has the ability to cast spells [CS-17].

This raises some questions: Is this what the embedded "soul" looks like in every Horcrux? Does the destruction of a Horcrux involve a confrontation with the piece of the soul of the wizard embedded within it? If so, presumably we would see Voldemort appear at various ages (the ages at which he made each Horcrux), meaning each subsequent "memory" or embodiment of Voldemort could be more dangerous.

Of course, the "memory" of Tom in the Diary could be a one-time thing, since we know that Voldemort gave it to Lucius Malfoy not just for safekeeping, but with the intention that it be smuggled into Hogwarts to be used in the reopening of the Chamber of Secrets [CS-17]. The one-seventh of Voldemort's soul contained therein worked from within the Diary, using it as a tool to enable the possession of the person who had custody of the Horcrux. This could be a clue that a Horcrux is dangerous to the one who possesses it -- and raises the question as to how dangerous it might have been for R.A.B. to possess the Locket Horcrux for the short time he did.

We can also put together some clues from the Diary episode to learn just a tiny bit about Horcrux creation. It seems clear that Moaning Myrtle's murder was the one Tom used to create his Horcrux. But Myrtle knows next to nothing about her own death [CS-16].

This seems to indicate that the creation of a Horcrux is an act separate from the murder that facilitates it, and is performed independently in time. We have corroboration from Tom himself regarding the deliberateness of Horcrux creation:

> "...I decided to leave behind a diary, preserving my sixteen-year-old self in its pages, so that one day, with luck, I would be able to lead another in my footsteps, and finish Salazar Slytherin's noble work." [CS-17]

Dumbledore, of course, recognizes this description by Riddle as referring to a Horcrux:

> "Well, although I did not see the Riddle who came out of

the diary, what you described to me was a phenomenon I had never witnessed. A mere memory starting to act and think for itself? A mere memory, sapping the life out of the girl into whose hands it had fallen? No, something much more sinister had lived inside that book.... a fragment of soul, I was almost sure of it. The diary had been a Horcrux." [HBP-23]

The Diary also provides us with our only opportunity to *see* the actual destruction of a Horcrux. It's encouraging to see that when Harry destroyed the diary, he destroyed the "memory" of Tom Riddle, that is, the one-seventh of Voldemort's soul preserved therein [CS-17]. It seems, then, that physical destruction of the Horcrux itself is enough to "kill" the embedded soul (though physical destruction of some of the remaining objects may be more difficult than was that of the Diary).

THE RING

We have as clean a chain of title for the Ring as we could possibly hope for. We first see the Ring when Dumbledore reveals it in response to Slughorn's comment about his withered hand. It's clear immediately that Slughorn recognizes the Ring (itself a set-up which is then paid off before *Half-Blood Prince* is over) [HBP-4]. The Ring at this point is cracked and destroyed.

We next see the Ring whole and undamaged when we journey through Dumbledore's Pensieve to the village of Little Hangleton. Marvolo identifies the Ring as a family heirloom, and mentions that it carries the Peverell coat of arms. (Since the Peverell family has never come up in any other context that I can recall, I assume this is not important.) [HBP-10].

The Ring next makes its appearance, still at Marvolo's house, when Tom Riddle returns to Little Hangleton to kill his father and grandparents. Then, lo and behold, it shows up on Tom's finger at a gathering of the Slug Club [HBP-17]. The Ring at this point is still undamaged. (Tom's soul, however, has to be in pretty ugly shape, given that we now know from the timeline he had already committed at least three murders while still in school!) It's pretty certain that Tom has not yet turned the Ring into a Horcrux at this point, because he is still gathering information from Slughorn on that very subject.

Finally, Dumbledore confirms to Harry that he did indeed destroy the Horcrux -- and with it, one-seventh of Voldemort's soul -- hidden inside the Ring [HBP-23], which Dumbledore found inside Marvolo's shack.

So with the Ring, we have a complete, beginning-to-end story of a Horcrux. While there won't be any payoffs for the Ring itself, because its story is over, we learn a couple of Horcrux-related facts that could be interesting.

For one thing, we learn that *creating* a Horcrux does not destroy the object in which the Horcrux is invested (this is corroborated by what we know of the Diary), but *destroying* it does. Does this mean that destruction of the object results in destruction of the Horcrux (as happened with the Diary)? Or is it the other way around: Destruction of the Horcrux results in destruction of the object (and we just didn't know what we were seeing in *Chamber of Secrets* -- note that a basilisk fang would certainly have killed any human).

It's also interesting to think of this in light of the theory that Harry is a Horcrux. Harry -- or his forehead, at least -- was damaged in what would have been the *creation* of the Horcrux (if he were such). This happenstance would contradict what we know of Horcrux creation based on our observation of the other Horcruxes Voldemort created. A small point, I know. We'll come back to touch on Harry-as-a-Horcrux later in Chapter 27.

THE LOCKET

We can trace the provenance of the Locket almost as cleanly as that of the Ring -- until it falls off the map.

We first see the Locket at Marvolo's shack, where Marvolo identifies it as a former possession of Salazar Slytherin himself [HBP-10]. Merope steals it, as we learn from Morfin [HBP-17]. We then trace it to Borgin and Burkes, where Caractacus Burke buys it from Merope for the rip-off price of 10 Galleons [HBP-13].

Voldemort actually finds it at Hepzibah Smith's, Hepzibah having bought it from Borgin and Burkes [HBP-20]. Voldemort murders Hepzibah, stealing not only the Locket but Hufflepuff's Cup as well, and poor bewitched house-elf Hokey takes the blame [HBP-20]. At some point subsequent to that, according to Dumbledore's well-researched conjectures, Voldemort turns the Locket into a Horcrux [HBP-23] and hides it in the Cave.

However, the chain of title breaks at this point. Dumbledore leads Harry to the Cave, takes the locket [HBP-26]. But the locket they fought so hard to take is a fake. According to the note left by R.A.B. (almost certainly Regulus Black), the Locket Horcrux has possibly already been destroyed, making Voldemort one step closer to being mortal again [HBP-28].

Note, by the way, the cost of destroying this particular Horcrux: R.A.B was still alive when he wrote the note announcing his intent to destroy the Horcrux, but knew that in destroying the Horcrux he faced death. (How did he expect his death to come? Through the act of destruction itself, just as destroying the Ring nearly killed Dumbledore? Or in retaliation by Voldemort? We can only wonder, at this point, and hope we learn more of this backstory in Book 7.)

It doesn't seem to have fully registered to Harry, by the way, that the Locket has possibly already been destroyed:

> *He kept reciting their names to himself, as though by listing them he could bring them within reach:* <u>*the locket... the cup... the snake... something of Gryffindor's or Ravenclaw's... the locket... the cup... the snake... something of Gryffindor's or Ravenclaw's...*</u> [HBP-30]

Or perhaps Harry is being justifiably cautious, wanting to *see* the destroyed Locket before striking it off his list. Which raises the obvious question: Where *is* the Locket?

Well, we have a nice potential set-up in *Order of the Phoenix*, when the trio is forced into cleaning up 12, Grimmauld Place:

> *....There was a musical box that emitted a faintly sinister, tinkling tune when wound, and they all found themselves becoming curiously weak and sleepy until Ginny had the sense to slam the lid shut; also a heavy locket that none of them could open, a number of ancient seals and, in a dusty box, an Order of Merlin, First Class, that had been awarded to Sirius's grandfather for "Services to the Ministry."* [OP-6].

Is this *the* Locket? Well, if I were Harry, *I'd* sure make a beeline for 12, Grimmauld Place to check it out. If Harry doesn't remember it, I'd bet Hermione does.

Is the Locket still there, however? We have set-ups that point us in two alternate directions for its location.

Kreacher, we know, has been smuggling his former mistress's treasures up into his own hiding places [OP-6]. Could he be keeping the Locket oh so safe elsewhere in the house?

We also learn, in *Half-Blood Prince*, that Mundungus Fletcher has been, in Dumbledore's words, "treating [Harry's] inheritance with light-fingered contempt" [HBP-12, 13]. (Presumably Dumbledore knows this from Aberforth, with whom Mundungus is meeting when Harry discovers him with a bag of contraband from Sirius's house.)

So did Mundungus steal the Locket? Very possible. Isn't it convenient, then, that Mundungus is nicely locked up in Azkaban where Harry can find him to question him?

The Kreacher payoff would be faster and easier, which could be a plus, given all the plot to be covered in Book 7. But for my money, the Mundungus payoff would be cooler, since it would take Harry inside Azkaban for the first time, and since it might force him to make the link that Aberforth Dumbledore is the Hog's Head barman. (And remember, Rowling has already said Dumbledore's family would be a profitable line of inquiry, so Harry and Aberforth must connect at *some* point in Book 7.)

CHAPTER 27

THE HORCRUXES WE DON'T KNOW

The subject of Horcruxes is like that squished animal on the side of the road. You don't want to look, you can't help it, and you feel sort of slimy afterwards.

That being said, let's wrap up with a look at the remaining Horcruxes. We've already discussed the two that have been destroyed -- the Diary and the Ring -- and the one that *may* have been destroyed -- the Locket. We know Voldemort split his soul into seven parts, encasing six of those parts in Horcruxes [HBP-23]. So let's look at the remaining three: The Cup. The Snake. And the one we're not sure about.

THE CUP

Much of the information we have about the Cup comes from the same sources we used in tracing the provenance of the Locket. We know Voldemort was first introduced to Helga Hufflepuff's cup at Hepzibah Smith's and that a "shadow" crossed his face when the cup was removed from his sight, indicating that it held significance for him [HBP-20]. Hepzibah was subsequently murdered, with her house-elf Hokey taking the blame. Along with Slytherin's Locket, the Cup disappeared from the Hepzibah Smith's house [HBP-20].

If we are to trust Dumbledore's research, we can assume the Cup was made into a Horcrux [HBP-23].

We have no other solid leads as to where the Cup might be... But Harry might have one path to journey down in his quest. Could Zacharias Smith, who is after all from Hufflepuff House, be related to Hepzibah? It's a good possibility.

So will Harry chase down Zacharias, get his cooperation somehow? Will Zacharias know the location of the Cup? Or at least some history that could lend us a clue?

And when Harry finds it, will he recognize it from having seen the memory in Dumbledore's Pensieve?

THE SNAKE

Dumbledore is convinced that Voldemort, lacking a better candidate, made Nagini into his last Horcrux. He gives his reasons so casually and quickly that it's easy to think they're a red herring rather than exposition on a silver platter:

> *"...I think I know what the sixth Horcrux is. I wonder what you will say when I confess that I have been curious for a while about the behavior of the snake, Nagini?"*

> *"The snake?" said Harry, startled. "You can use animals as Horcruxes?"*

> *"Well, it is inadvisable to do so," said Dumbledore, "because to confide a part of your soul to something that can think and move for itself is obviously a very risky business. However, if my calculations are correct, Voldemort was still at least one Horcrux short of his goal of six when he entered your parents'*

house with the intention of killing you.... I am sure that he was intending to make his final Horcrux with your death.

"As we know, he failed. After an interval of some years, however, he used Nagini to kill an old Muggle man, and it might then have occurred to him to turn her into his last Horcrux. She underlines the Slytherin connection, which enhances Lord Voldemort's mystique; I think he is perhaps as fond of her as he can be of anything; he certainly likes to keep her close, and he seems to have an unusual amount of control over her, even for a Parselmouth. " [HBP-23]

With Dumbledore's reasoning in mind, let's look back at that mysterious incident after Nagini attacked Mr. Weasley. Dumbledore is fiddling with one of his curious silver instruments:

The instrument tinkled into life at once with rhythmic clinking noises. Tiny puffs of pale green smoke issued from the minuscule silver tube at the top. Dumbledore watched the smoke closely, his brow furrowed, and after a few seconds, the tiny puffs became a steady stream of smoke that thickened and coiled in the air.... A serpent's head grew out of the end of it, opening its mouth wide. Harry wondered whether the instrument was confirming his story: He looked eagerly at Dumbledore for a sign that he was right, but Dumbledore did not look up.

"Naturally, naturally," murmured Dumbledore apparently to himself, still observing the stream of smoke without the slightest sign of surprise. "But in essence divided?"

Harry could make neither head nor tail of this question. The smoke serpent, however, split itself instantly into two snakes, both coiling and undulating in the dark air. With a look of grim satisfaction Dumbledore gave the instrument another gentle tap with his wand: The clinking noise slowed and died, and the

smoke serpents grew faint, became a formless haze, and vanished.
[OP-22]

What did Dumbledore learn from this little experiment? Let's detour over to see how someone else interpreted what happened with Nagini that night:

> *"You seem to have visited the snake's mind because that was where the Dark Lord was at that particular moment," snarled Snape. "He was possessing the snake at the time and so you dreamed you were inside it too...."*[OP-24]

Snape, working on the best information available to him, assumes Voldemort was *possessing* Nagini at the moment of attack.

However, I think Snape was wrong. I think Dumbledore's experiment shows that Voldemort and Nagini were *not* one and the same at that moment, that while Voldemort was certainly *controlling* her, he was *not* possessing Nagini. They were, in fact, "in essence divided." Voldemort remained within his own body -- but the one-seventh of Voldemort's soul that was already in Nagini's body was in charge. (How is this possible? Remember what we learned from the Diary about the ability of Horcruxes to take independent action.)

I think Nagini as a Horcrux will provide us with some terrific action in Book 7. Think how much is made of the fact that Harry is a Parselmouth. Lots of set-up, and yes, we saw a significant payoff for this in *Chamber of Secrets.* So is the Parseltongue storyline over?

I don't think so. We were reminded of the significance of Parseltongue in *Half-Blood Prince* when we visited the Gaunt family. Because of this *re*-set-up, I would almost guarantee we will see Harry using his Parseltongue abilities in Book 7.

How will he use them? To talk privately to Voldemort?

Perhaps. Or could we instead see a confrontation or battle involving Nagini in Book 7? If so, wouldn't it make sense for Harry to attempt to control her using Parseltongue? (And what happens if others are around and don't understand what's happening?) Now *that's* a scene I want to see!

IS HARRY A HORCRUX?

In discussing the Sixth Horcrux, we must start by addressing one of the most-discussed questions in Potterdom: Is Harry a Horcrux? ("Harry" in this instance would include any *part* of Harry, notably his scar.)

The strongest argument *for* this rests in the odd psychic relationship forged between Harry and Voldemort through Harry's curse scar.

> *"Voldemort put a bit of himself in* me?*" Harry said, thunderstruck.*

> *"It certainly seems so."* [CS-18]

And the "weird connection" [OP-18] between Harry and Voldemort bothers Harry greatly.

I do not believe, however, that Harry, or any part of him (such as his scar) is a Horcrux. The Harry-Voldemort connection, weird though it may be, is something different.

For one thing, *Dumbledore* doesn't think Harry is a Horcrux. As he lays out all his Horcrux information [HBP-23], he never mentions this even as a remote possibility to Harry.

Could Dumbledore be wrong? Possibly, but *extremely* unlikely, given the amount of time and energy he has devoted both to the subject of Voldemort's Horcruxes, and to Harry's relationship with Voldemort.

Yes, Dumbledore does have a history of withholding information from Harry. He withheld the full story of Harry's parents' death, he withheld the information regarding the Prophecy. And, most notably, in *Half-Blood Prince*, he withheld the information regarding Snape's involvement with the Prophecy.

We can perhaps understand why he did this last. Dumbledore was trying to preserve (the remains of) Harry's relationship with Snape. (Let's stop to ask: Why? Why would Dumbledore consider that relationship worth preserving?)

However, regarding the Horcruxes, Dumbledore has been more open than we have ever seen him before. For Dumbledore to suspect that Harry is a Horcrux at this point and not tell him, not even hint, would go far beyond the mere withholding of information. It would amount to Dumbledore lying to Harry, deliberately misleading him as to what the sixth Horcrux is. And I do not believe Dumbledore would do that.

We have further evidence that Harry is not a Horcrux in Voldemort's repeated attempts to kill Harry. Why would he kill the vessel in which a precious one-seventh of his soul resides? That would make *no* sense whatsoever!

Ah, I hear you murmur, but what if Voldemort doesn't *know* he made Harry into a Horcrux?

Sorry, but I don't think that idea holds up under scrutiny. Every indication we have is that the creation of a Horcrux is a very intentional act, with specific spells needed to create it. Voldemort came to Godric's Hollow to kill Harry, responding to his understanding of the Prophecy. He certainly wouldn't have cast the Horcrux spell by mistake at that moment! And even if a Horcrux *could* be made inadvertently, wouldn't Voldemort have noticed one-seventh of his soul missing when he went to create Nagini as his final Horcrux?

And let's look at Nagini-the-Horcrux again. Voldemort has control over her. But he has no such control over Harry -- the best he can do is try to infiltrate his mind by planting dreams and visions by stealth. Clearly the Harry-Voldemort relationship is of a different ilk than the Nagini-Voldemort relationship. (And do we really think Occlumency could work at all as a barrier to prevent Voldemort from meddling with Harry's mind, as Dumbledore and Snape expected it to, if Voldemort was *inside* Harry?)

Final evidence against the possibility of Harry (or his scar) being a Horcrux comes from J.K. Rowling herself. On her website (in the "Rumours" section), we recently saw the following interchange:

[Rumour:] The Sorting Hat is a Horcrux.

[Rowling:] No, it isn't. Horcruxes do not draw attention to themselves by singing songs in front of large audiences.

The Sorting Hat would be a most dangerous Horcrux, this answer implies, because of its ability to communicate. That in turn implies that, were the Sorting Hat a Horcrux, it would *know* it was, and would be able to communicate that fact.

Presumably the same applies to Harry. And let's remember what Dumbledore said about it being dangerous to make a Horcrux of something that can "think and move for itself." Harry, of course, can do more than that.

Yes, Harry and Voldemort have a strange psychic connection. But no, Harry is not the Sixth Horcrux. (And neither is his scar.)

So what *is* the remaining Horcrux? Let's go back to Dumbledore's conclusions.

SOMETHING OF GRYFFINDOR'S OR RAVENCLAW'S?

We don't have a lot of obvious candidates here. (Perhaps the lack of candidates is what causes so many people to speculate as far afield as Peter Pettigrew's silver hand!) But Dumbledore speculated that the Sixth Horcrux would be something belonging to Gryffindor or Ravenclaw. So let's do what Harry is likely to do, and follow Dumbledore's lead.

We know next to nothing about Rowena Ravenclaw, so if it's something of hers, it will have to wait until Book 7 for us to discover the actual object, I would think. Or we could find that the Horcrux is an object we've seen before, but learn only in Book 7 of its relationship to Ravenclaw.

For instance, some have speculated that the wand we saw in Ollivander's shop window in *Sorcerer's Stone* could have been Ravenclaw's, and could now be Voldemort's Horcrux. An interesting idea -- though I have to say, especially given the protection put around the Locket, the front window of a shop in Diagon Alley strikes me as a very iffy storage location for something so valuable!

Nevertheless, if we should learn early in Book 7 that an object we are already familiar with once belonged to Rowena Ravenclaw, we should sit up sharp and take notice -- because it's likely to be very important indeed.

We also know comparatively little about Godric Gryffindor. The Sorting Hat was his, but Rowling has taken that off the table as a potential Horcrux.

Could the Horcrux be Gryffindor's Sword that Harry pulled out of the Hat when fighting the basilisk in *Chamber of Secrets*? Perhaps. But if so, how would Voldemort have contaminated that Sword? We have no evidence that it ever appeared in Dumbledore's office until after the basilisk was killed. Still, it's a possibility.

Could Voldemort have taken the object to Godric's Hollow when he went to kill Harry? Possible. But would it still be there 17 years later? And would Harry recognize what it was? ...A lot of obstacles to this possibility, but we *are* going to Godric's Hollow in Book 7, and presumably we will learn something of interest there.

I want to propose one more possibility, based on Dumbledore's pointing out that Tom Riddle liked to collect trophies even before he knew he was a wizard [HBP-13, 23]. What about that Special Award for Services to the School? It's originally set up when Ron vomits slugs on it in detention [CS-7]. The seeming payoff would be when Ron realizes the award was given to Tom Riddle [CS-13]. But this is the only object belonging to Voldemort we know of that isn't in his possession -- and it's certainly in a very safe place: A trophy room no one ever goes in, in the most heavily defended building in all of Britain!

We don't *have* all the set-ups we need to answer the Horcrux questions. But if we had them, if Book 7 was that highly predictable, wouldn't we all be pretty bored?

CHAPTER 28

HOW SAFE IS HOGWARTS?

Hogwarts is the safest place in the Wizarding World, we are repeatedly told. It is protected not only by walls and gates, but by enchantments to keep people from entering by stealth [PA-9]:

> *"...the walls and grounds of Hogwarts are guarded by many ancient spells and charms to ensure the bodily and mental safety of those who dwell within them," said Snape.* [OP-24]

In addition, Hogwarts is Unplottable; it can't be mapped or found with a map. It's bewitched to look like a dangerous old ruin, the better to keep Muggles away [GF-11].

APPARITION AND PORTKEYS

We're also told -- over and over and over -- that it's impossible to Apparate into Hogwarts or to Disapparate from it [HBP-18].

> *"As you may know, it is usually impossible to Apparate or Disapparate within Hogwarts. The headmaster has lifted this enchantment, purely within the Great Hall, for one hour, so as to enable you to practice. May I emphasize that you will not be able to Apparate outside the walls of this Hall, and that you would be*

unwise to try." [HBP-18]

Hermione gets downright exasperated repeating this to Ron and Harry -- and to us. If ever a set-up was drummed into our heads, this is it.

But is it true?

We already see some cracks in the Apparition rule. The House-Elves, we learn quickly, can Apparate within Hogwarts. J.K. Rowling explains this as necessary for their duties. Okay, that's fine. No breach of security there.

But House-Elves can apparently Apparate *into* Hogwarts as well, as we see when Dumbledore sends Kreacher there [HBP-3]. Was it Dumbledore's magic that was working there, rather than Kreacher's? Even if that's the case, if Dumbledore can send something (or someone) into Hogwarts, mightn't another wizard be able to do so?

House-Elves aren't the only creature able to Apparate in and out of Hogwarts. As we see when Dumbledore uses Fawkes as an early warning system against Umbridge, Fawkes is easily able to Apparate around the castle [OP-22]. Even more impressive -- Fawkes Apparates Dumbledore entirely out of Hogwarts after Dumbledore Stuns the room full of Aurors and Umbridgites [OP-27]. (Again, we simply don't know: Was this Fawkes's magic or Dumbledore's at work?)

But what about wizards? Let's face it, if you're told over and over and over again that you can't possibly Apparate at Hogwarts... *and* you're warned of vague but horrible things happening if you try... *and* you see someone get splinched (which probably happens at least once in every Apparition class)... Well, you're darned unlikely to even try!

Let's think about Montague for a minute. Stuck in the Vanishing Cabinet, he managed to Apparate out [HBP-27]. But where was the "inside" of the Vanishing Cabinet at the time (or more accurately the magical "tunnel" between the two Cabinets)? We know Montague traveled magically back and forth between Hogwarts and Borgin and Burkes, based on what Montague was able to overhear from within the Cabinet. So there's a 50% possibility that he was actually within Hogwarts when he Apparated out of the cabinet.

And in any event, he ended up *in* Hogwarts, in a fourth floor bathroom. So no matter how you look at it, Montague either Apparated *within* Hogwarts, or *from* Borgin & Burkes *to* Hogwarts.

Can't Apparate in Hogwarts? So they say. But should we believe it?

How will we find out the truth? Well, it won't be via Hermione, I'll bet. She's the one who's been telling us lo these many books that Apparition is impossible in Hogwarts. Hermione believes what she reads, believes what she's told, and doesn't break rules without great provocation.

But Harry... I can easily see several situations in which Harry, who has announced he's not going back to Hogwarts as a student, might need to get into the school by stealth. He might want to chat with Dumbledore's portrait. He might want access to Dumbledore's Pensieve. He might want to get the Half-Blood Prince's old potions book out of that carefully-marked cabinet in the Room of Requirement...

Can't you just see Harry, unable to figure out another way in, announcing that he'll Apparate in (to Hermione's shocked gasps and warnings)? After all, Harry was there on the Lightning-Struck Tower. He heard Draco's whole story about what Montague did. He has all the information he needs to figure it out, and the courage to try it.

Am I ready to put money on this as a bona fide prediction? Not quite. But I'm close to it...

Traveling by Portkey isn't quite the same as Apparition, but were I on the board of Hogwarts, I would certainly insist on it being impossible to enter or leave the school by Portkey. Yet Dumbledore does both, sending Harry and the Weasley kids *from* Hogwarts to 12, Grimmauld Place by Portkey [OP-22], and sending Harry *to* Hogwarts by Portkey after the battle at the Ministry of Magic [OP-36].

Again, we're looking at Dumbledore's magic. Since he's responsible for much of the magic protecting Hogwarts, one might think he would be able to waive those protections for his own purposes.

However, Dumbledore's not the only wizard who can use a Portkey to get in and out of Hogwarts. In *Goblet of Fire*, Barty Crouch, Jr. (posing as Fake Moody) sends Harry and Cedric out of Hogwarts when he turns the Triwizard Cup into a Portkey -- then Harry uses the Portkey to return to Hogwarts once again.

If that isn't a breach of security, I don't know what is.

OTHER SECURITY MEASURES

Despite all the ballyhooing about the safety of Hogwarts throughout the books, the castle can't possibly be quite as safe as one might wish. Because every time there's a new threat, new security measures are taken, measures that shouldn't have been needed if the place was really as safe as it was trumpeted to be in the first place.

As early as *Prisoner of Azkaban*, Mr. Weasley is convinced that Sirius Black, having been able to break out of Azkaban, will be able to break into Hogwarts [PA-4]. He's not the only one who thinks this, so new security is added: Dementors are stationed as guards around the school just in case he tries [PA-4]. (Apparently no one bothered to think: If Sirius Black could get past the dementors at Azkaban, wouldn't he be able to elude them at Hogwarts?)

After Voldemort returns to his body (and after the Ministry of Magic admits as much), security is beefed up *again*. The gates are bewitched by Dumbledore to remain locked in the face of *alohomora* spells. Anti-intruder jinxes are laid on the walls to make them unclimbable [HBP-8]. A complex array of countercurses are laid in, and a band of Aurors is assigned to the school [HBP-3]. We also learn Dumbledore lays in extra security whenever he leaves the school [HBP-25]. Nevertheless, again, the same people who insist all this security will be adequate don't seem all that confident in it, as they warn students to report anything suspicious [HBP-8].

And as we see in *Half-Blood Prince*, all these security measures *weren't* enough to protect against Draco's clever attack from within [HBP-19].

Why does it matter, you ask? After all, Harry has already announced his intention not to return to Hogwarts.

Maybe he won't go back as a student. But I have to believe that he *will* go back. *Harry Potter* is too firmly centered in Hogwarts to abandon its patterns completely in Book 7. Hogwarts is just too important to Harry -- and to Voldemort.

In fact, I wouldn't be surprised if a major battle of Book 7 -- perhaps even *the* final battle -- takes place as a fight for Hogwarts itself.

The security barrier around Hogwarts has already shown itself to be porous. But a new factor was introduced at the end of *Half-Blood Prince:* How secure is Hogwarts now, we must ask, with Dumbledore gone?

DUMBLEDORE'S PRESENCE

Dumbledore is inexorably linked with the safety of Hogwarts [SS-4, CS-17, OP-28, HBP-11].

> *"I reckon the staff are safer than most people while Dumbledore's headmaster; he's supposed to be the only one Voldemort ever feared, isn't he?" Harry went on.* [HBP-4]

We're also warned quite early on that Hogwarts is less safe when Dumbledore is not there:

> *"We're in trouble now," [Hagrid] said hoarsely. "No Dumbledore. They might as well close the school tonight. There'll be an attack a day with him gone."* [CS-14]

But Dumbledore *is* gone. He's gone forever. So what does that mean to the enchantments placed to ensure the safety of Hogwarts?

We know Dumbledore himself cast many of the enchantments protecting Hogwarts -- we see him release some of those spells when he and Harry fly over the walls, racing to the Dark Mark [HBP-27].

What happens to those spells now that the spellcaster is dead? We have an ominous clue from Harry:

> *He had known there was no hope from the moment that the full Body-Bind Curse Dumbledore had placed upon him lifted, known that it could have happened only because its caster was*

dead... [HBP-28]

Will Dumbledore's protective spells around Hogwarts also be lifted? Yes, I realize that if they are, other professors are able to cast some of those spells... But it has been made clear for so long that Dumbledore's presence is linked to Hogwarts' safety. Therefore I believe Hogwarts will be in dire danger in Book 7 as a result of Dumbledore's untimely death.

UNITY BETWEEN THE HOUSES

What other defense does the school have against its enemies? Drawing on what seems a purely thematic subplot, it may be that unity among the houses could provide some protection.

The Sorting Hat hints as much:

Oh, know the perils, read the signs,
The warning history shows,
For our Hogwarts is in danger
From external, deadly foes
And we must unite inside her
Or we'll crumble from within
I have told you, I have warned you....
Let the Sorting now begin. [OP-11]

Who's likely to heed the Hat, though? What with the inter-House rivalry for the House Cup, the Quidditch Cup and the like, not to mention the specific animosity between Gryffindor and Slytherin, unity would seem to be far from the students' minds.

Except for Hermione. *She* gets it. She's been a promoter of unity in general since she took up S.P.E.W. She considers S.P.E.W. so important, in fact, she would even consider it as a career once she leaves Hogwarts [OP-11]. She also specifically stresses the need for inter-House unity [OP-11]. Could Hermione play a major role in bringing Hogwarts together to fight those "external deadly foes"? She has certainly been set up to do so, for many books now.

One other person understood the need for unity, of course: Dumbledore. We see this when he invites the foreign students to rally at Hogwarts in the wake of Lord Voldemort's return:

> *"Every guest in this Hall,"* said Dumbledore, and his eyes *lingered upon the Durmstrang students, "will be welcomed back here at any time, should they wish to come. I say to you all, once again -- in the light of Lord Voldemort's return, we are only as strong as we are united, as weak as we are divided. Lord Voldemort's gift for spreading discord and enmity is very great. We can fight it only by showing an equally strong bond of friendship and trust."* [GF-37]

Once again we see that the greatest weapon against Voldemort is love.

But with Dumbledore gone, and unity hard to come by, how safe is Hogwarts in Book 7? My feeling, given the set-ups we have... Not very.

CHAPTER 29

MORE MAGICAL LOCATIONS

Other than Hogwarts, only a very few other locations might hold interest for Harry or Voldemort.

12, GRIMMAULD PLACE

The future of 12, Grimmauld Place hung in the balance at the beginning of *Half-Blood Prince*. With Sirius's death and Harry's inheritance of the house, Dumbledore appeared understandably concerned about whether Harry's inheritance would stand. He validated this by showing that Kreacher, much as he might *wish* to serve Bellatrix rather than Harry, had to do Harry's bidding [HBP-3]. According to Dumbledore, this proves Harry owns 12, Grimmauld Place.

But it's interesting that Dumbledore didn't *know* the answer to the inheritance question without performing his test:

> "...The situation is fraught with complications. We do not know whether the enchantments we ourselves have placed upon it, for example, making it Unplottable, will hold now that ownership has passed from Sirius's hands..." [HBP-3]

This raises the question: If the death of the owner meant so much to the continuation of the enchantments guarding the house, what does the death of the Secret Keeper mean?

Dumbledore was the Secret Keeper regarding the location of 12, Grimmauld Place. No one was able even to find the place unless Dumbledore told them how personally [OP-6]. We know from James and Lily Potter's death how crucial a Secret Keeper can be. (Note that once again the Secret being Kept involves a location. And remember that Dumbledore himself offered to be the Potters' Secret Keeper -- an indication of how important he considered the Secret of location [PA-10].)

So what happens now that Dumbledore is dead? Does 12, Grimmauld Place become Plottable? Is it visible from the street (to the great shock of the neighbors)? Can it be entered by anyone who chooses to do so?

Given that even Dumbledore didn't know the answers to the questions regarding Harry's inheritance, I suspect the members of the Order of the Phoenix may not know the answers to all of these questions. But will they realize that the questions must be asked? (After all, it was Dumbledore who masterminded the Order's moving-out when Sirius died.)

Why would Voldemort or any Death Eaters *want* to get into 12, Grimmauld Place, anyway? I can think of a couple of reasons. First, obviously, it's the headquarters of the Order of the Phoenix. Being able to enter the house could mean catching members of the Order. It could also mean finding any clues or evidence or plans they might have left behind or stored there.

Second, there could be some serious Dark goodies stored away at the old Black mansion. We saw some of what Sirius and the trio, under the supervision of Mrs. Weasley, managed to clean out: Daggers, claws, snakeskins, magical boxes, "tweezers" that attacked

Harry, a mysterious bottle of blood... [OP-6]

And oh, yeah, that gold locket. Hmm. Wonder if there's anyone who might want to check on the security of *that* little item?

As mentioned in Chapter 23, 12, Grimmauld Place has been partially looted already, first by Kreacher (in which case his treasures are probably still in the house) [OP-23], and then by Mundungus (in which case, who knows?) [HBP-13]. These lootings could turn out to be a blessing in disguise if indeed the house is open to all comers in Book 7.

In any event, I think Harry *must* return to 12, Grimmauld Place in Book 7. Otherwise, why would the inheritance questions even have been raised?

Another place in which both Voldemort and Harry have shared mutual interest:

THE DEPARTMENT OF MYSTERIES

We spent a lot of time in the Department of Mysteries in *Order of the Phoenix*, and explored a lot further than just the Hall of Prophecies. We learned the Unspeakables study the Mysteries of Time, Thought, Death [OP-34], and the Universe [OP-35], as well as Prophecy. And they study the Mystery of Love:

> *"There is a room in the Department of Mysteries,"* interrupted Dumbledore, *"that is kept locked at all times. It contains a force that is at once more wonderful and more terrible than death, than human intelligence, than forces of nature. It is also, perhaps, the most mysterious of the many subjects for study that reside there. It is the power held within that room that you possess in such quantities and which Voldemort has not at all.*

That power took you to save Sirius tonight. That power also saved you from possession by Voldemort, because he could not bear to reside in a body so full of the force he detests. In the end, it mattered not that you could not close your mind. It was your heart that saved you." [OP-37]

Harry may have gotten tired of Dumbledore saying he would defeat Voldemort by love in *Half-Blood Prince*. But in Book 7, might he feel he needs to learn a little more about what Dumbledore was always talking about?

Maybe he can, if he remembers that locked door [OP-34] at the Department of Mysteries. There are people who might be able to answer Harry's questions about this force "more wonderful and more terrible than death," if he thinks to ask the questions in the first place.

So while I don't feel that the Department of Mysteries is a "must-visit" location for Book 7 in the way that Hogwarts and 12, Grimmauld Place are, I wouldn't be at all surprised if we paid a visit.

There is one location that we have *never* visited through the entire series, though we certainly know a good deal about it:

AZKABAN

Azkaban, the wizard prison, is by all accounts a horrible place:

"Azkaban must be terrible," Harry muttered. Lupin nodded grimly.

"The fortress is set on a tiny island, way out to sea, but they don't need walls and water to keep the prisoners in, not when they're all trapped inside their own heads, incapable of a single

cheerful thought. Most of them go mad within weeks." [PA-10]

And that's an account from someone who's never been there. Accounts from those who have been inside corroborate the place's awfulness:

> *"He wasn't the only one," said Sirius bitterly. "Most go mad in there, and plenty stop eating in the end. They lose the will to live. You could always tell when a death was coming, because the dementors could sense it, they got excited..."* [GF-27]

So why would we care about Azkaban in Book 7? Well, some notable prisoners are currently housed there: Mundungus Fletcher and Lucius Malfoy.

Lucius was sent to Azkaban after being captured in the Battle at the Ministry of Magic at the end of *Order of the Phoenix* [OP-38]. Not that Harry cares about that. Azkaban is the right place for Lucius, and may he stay there a long, long time.

But Mundungus is very possibly somebody Harry might want to track down, given the likelihood that he stole the Locket Horcrux from 12, Grimmauld Place [HBP-12]. If Harry visits Grimmauld Place, searches Kreacher's hidey-holes, and finds the Locket gone, the next logical place to go is Azkaban to ask Mundungus where it is.

Sneaking in to Azkaban may not be such an issue anymore now that the Dementors are gone [OP-38]. In fact, one has to wonder why Lucius and Mundungus haven't broken out themselves, since the horror of Azkaban seemed to be rooted in the presence of the Dementors.

It's possible that if we go to Azkaban, we will find it a shell of its former self for this reason (not that that would be a bad thing).

GODRIC'S HOLLOW

There is one other "must-visit" location for Book 7, tossed off as almost an afterthought in the very last pages of *Half-Blood Prince*:

> *"I thought I might go back to Godric's Hollow," Harry muttered. He had had the idea in his head ever since the night of Dumbledore's death. "For me, it started there, all of it. I've just got a feeling I need to go there. And I can visit my parents' graves, I'd like that."* [HBP-30]

What will Harry find there? We really have no idea whatsoever, do we? It's actually quite remarkable that we started six books ago with the deaths of Lily and James, that we've heard so much about them, that so much depends on what happened there... and yet that we have virtually no set-ups about what Harry might find there.

But I'm sure we can all agree that whatever he finds will be important.

CHAPTER 30

THE UNFORGIVABLE CURSES

When looking at spells and potions that yield dramatic set-ups and payoffs, first and foremost we have to examine the Unforgivable Curses, especially the Imperius Curse and the Cruciatus Curse.

THE IMPERIUS CURSE

The Imperius Curse has given the Ministry of Magic trouble in the past, we learn from Fake-Moody in *Goblet of Fire* [GF-14]. Back in Voldemort's first heyday, the Ministry couldn't figure out who was doing bad things out of their own free will, and who had been Imperiused into doing them.

We get a set-up in *Order of the Phoenix* that we might be in for some Imperius action in the near future when Harry wonders if the Death Eaters have put the Imperius Curse on Lucius Malfoy [OP-9]. This is no more than a nice little mention, something to remind us that this Curse, which allows the spellcaster total control of the victim, is still out there, still a threat.

That tiny set-up gets a pretty full payoff in *Half-Blood Prince* when Katie Bell is Imperiused to get her to carry the deadly necklace into Hogwarts [HBP-13]. We actually learn quite a lot about the Imperius Curse if we look at this incident closely.

First, we learn Madam Rosmerta was the one who cast the curse on Katie -- but Rosmerta was *herself* under the Imperius Curse at the time! This tells us that someone under the Imperius Curse can actually *cast* the Curse, which would seem to allow the original spellcaster enormous amounts of power.

We also know that, in *Goblet of Fire*, Viktor Krum was Imperiused into performing the Cruciatus Curse on Fleur during the Third Task [GF-31]. Can we therefore assume that someone can be Imperiused into casting the final Unforgivable Curse -- Avada Kedavra? If so, the caster of the Imperius Curse is in a position to go around killing people without ever being linked to the crimes.

Note that we also have a pattern forming here: We've now seen an Imperiused wizard or witch perform two of the three Unforgivable Curses. Therefore I wouldn't be surprised if in Book 7 we see the obvious third part to the pattern: Someone Imperiused into performing Avada Kedavra. Should we see an unexpected murder from a highly unexpected source, let's keep that in mind.

(We must ask the question: Did we already see just this payoff in Snape's killing of Dumbledore? I would say not. I think Snape knew exactly what he was doing -- even if *we* may not know exactly what that was yet.)

What else do we learn about the Imperius Curse from the Katie Bell/Madam Rosmerta episode? We learn the spell can stay in effect over a fairly extended period of time. We also learn the spellcaster doesn't have to be physically present for the spell to continue to work (as Fake-Moody was present when Viktor was Imperiused). No wonder the Ministry has had so much trouble with this curse!

Another lesson from this episode, and one the characters would do well to heed: We now know that when someone is

Imperiused, it's important to sit down right away and figure out who performed the Curse.

Hermione is on the right track when she figures out it must be a woman who cast it, given that Katie Bell received the necklace in the ladies' room of the Three Broomsticks [HBP-24]. But she shouldn't have let it sit there. If only everyone had thought through what Hermione just said, and moved on to ask the obvious question: What woman is most likely to be in the ladies' room at the Three Broomsticks?... the cursing of Madam Rosmerta might have been solved much earlier.

Dumbledore does figure it out, of course, moments before his death [HBP-27]. But it's a little late. Let's hope the characters learn the lesson we've just learned: When someone is under the Imperius Curse, find out who cast it!... A potentially important lesson, if indeed Book 7 fills out the 1-2-3 pattern set up in *Order of the Phoenix* and *Half-Blood Prince* by having someone cast Avada Kedavra while under the Imperius Curse.

We also learn from the Rosmerta episode, incidentally, that Draco Malfoy is a much better wizard than we might have expected, to cast an Unforgivable and produce such exact behavior as a result.

Or is it that Draco is just average, and the problem is that Rosmerta is especially weak?

This matters, because while the Imperius Curse may be Unforgivable, it is not unbeatable. We learn from Fake-Moody that people with strength of character *can* fight the Curse.

We see that Harry *can* fight the Curse right away, when Fake-Moody teaches it [GF-15]. This set-up is paid off when Harry manages to fight the Curse when Voldemort himself casts it in the graveyard [GF-34].

This provides a hint we can use if we find Imperiused people running around Book 7. Who is weak enough to be used and manipulated in this way? (Percy comes to mind. Also Slughorn. Trelawney. Pettigrew. Crabbe and Goyle. Go ahead, add to the list.) It also can help us figure out who might *not* be easily Imperiused -- McGonagall, Neville, Snape. Something to keep in mind for Book 7.

It is interesting, by the way, that Harry can fight against the Imperius Curse, and he seems to have beat back Avada Kedavra as an infant, but he appears to be helpless in the face of...

THE CRUCIATUS CURSE

The Cruciatus Curse has a special appeal to Harry from the moment he hears of it. Only four chapters after first learning about it, he begins to fantasize about perfecting the Curse on Snape [GF-18] (A nice foreshadowing of his later attempts to cast the Curse on Snape in *Half-Blood Prince!*).

Harry is nonetheless shocked to see Viktor perform the Cruciatus Curse on Fleur in the Third Task [GF-31] -- again, a good set-up, because it lets us see what happens when the victim is a human rather than a spider. We also begin to learn in *Goblet of Fire* and much more in *Order of the Phoenix* what the consequences of the Cruciatus Curse can be, as we learn of, then witness, the insanity of Neville's parents.

The Cruciatus Curse is Harry's go-to when he wants to really harm someone he really hates. He tries it first on Bellatrix in the Battle at the Ministry:

Hatred rose in Harry such as he had never known before. He flung himself out from behind the fountain and bellowed "Crucio!"

Bellatrix screamed. The spell had knocked her off her feet, but she did not writhe and shriek with pain as Neville had -- she was already on her feet again, breathless, no longer laughing. Harry dodged behind the golden fountain again -- her counterspell hit the head of the handsome wizard, which was blown off and landed twenty feet away, gouging long scratches into the wooden floor.

"Never used an Unforgivable Curse before, have you, boy?" she yelled. She had abandoned her baby voice now. "You need to <u>mean</u> them, Potter! You need to really want to cause pain -- to enjoy it -- righteous anger won't hurt me for long -- I'll show you how it is done, shall I? I'll give you a lesson--" [OP-36]

We hear much the same response in *Half-Blood Prince* when Harry tries to use the Cruciatus Curse on Snape, and Snape blocks him:

Twenty yards apart, [Snape] and Harry looked at each other before raising their wands simultaneously.

"<u>Cruc</u>--"

But Snape parried the curse, knocking Harry backward off his feet before he could complete it; Harry rolled over and scrambled back up again as the huge Death Eater behind him yelled, "<u>Incendio</u>!" Harry heard an explosive bang and a dancing orange light spilled over all of them: Hagrid's house was on fire.

"Fang's in there, yer evil--!" Hagrid bellowed.

"<u>Cruc</u>--" yelled Harry for the second time, aiming for the figure ahead illuminated in the dancing firelight, but Snape blocked the spell again. Harry could see him sneering.
"No Unforgivable Curses from you, Potter!" he shouted over

the rushing of the flames, Hagrid's yells, and the wild yelping of the trapped Fang. "You haven't got the nerve or the ability--" [HBP-28]

(Note, by the way, that Harry, perhaps unconsciously, follows Snape's advice. He next tries to cast Incarcerous, Stupefy, Impedimenta, Sectumsempra, and Levicorpus -- but he does not try an Unforgivable again.)

From these two incidents, we learn that blinding hatred isn't enough to successfully cast an Unforgivable -- because Harry certainly has enough of *that* to go around in both cases! Apparently one needs nerve, ability, and the enjoyment of causing pain to successfully cast an Unforgivable... All prerequisites that Draco *does* possess.

Will Harry successfully cast the Cruciatus Curse? I think that depends on what "Unforgivable" means.

So far, all we know is that casting an Unforgivable Curse on a human lands one in Azkaban. But "Unforgivable" is a pretty strong term, even for a crime carrying a prison sentence. *Who* is refusing to forgive? Is it just the Wizengamot? Or are there deeper, more spiritual consequences of casting an Unforgivable?

We know from Slughorn's memory about Horcruxes [HBP-23] that *"Killing rips the soul apart."* This tells us casting the Avada Kedavra does indeed cause harm to the spellcaster. Is this true for all the Unforgivables? Would it harm Harry's soul in some way to successfully cast "Crucio"?

The answer to the question doesn't necessarily make our predictions for Book 7 any easier. If the answer is "Yes, it would harm Harry's soul," I don't think that would prevent J.K. Rowling from having Harry successfully cast it. As Harry's face is scarred, so his soul could be scarred by the successful casting of an Unforgivable -- a consequence he would have to live with and deal with.

So I don't know if Harry will *land* "Crucio" in Book 7. But I would bet a large sum of money that he will *try* to cast the curse. And given that once again we have a 1-2-3 pattern, I would expect that he *will* successfully cast it.

Whom will he cast it on? Not on Snape, is my guess. I don't think Harry can beat Snape wand-to-wand. My guess would be Draco.

One last Unforgivable Curse to give at least a quick glance to:

THE AVADA KEDAVRA

We have all realized, haven't we, that "Avada Kedavra" is etymologically related to "abracadabra"? Very clever to combine that with Latin roots meaning, approximately, "become a cadaver."

Avada Kedavra will at least put in an appearance in Book 7, as we have a very important question to be answered: How did Harry beat the Killing Curse as an infant?

But will we see the curse cast? I think we will, as a payoff to one (or both) of two set-ups already provided. One I mentioned above: The fulfillment of the pattern of Imperiused wizards casting Unforgivable Curses.

The other set-up involves Draco's inability to cast the Avada Kedavra curse on Dumbledore [HBP-27]. I suspect Draco may try again. Whether he succeeds depends, I think, on his redeemability. If we see him succeed, we will know that his soul is indeed, "ripped apart..." in which case I expect we can count on a very bad end for

Draco.

CHAPTER 31

THE DRAUGHT OF LIVING DEATH

We first hear about the Draught of Living Death in Harry's first Potions class with Snape [SS-8]. At the time it seemed like a throwaway. But as I mentioned in Chapter 24, haven't we all realized everything in that class was a set-up in one form or another?

Let's eavesdrop on that class closely for a second, as Potions Master Snape grills his least favorite student:

> *"Potter!" said Snape suddenly. "What would I get if I added powdered root of asphodel to an infusion of wormwood?"*

> *Powdered root of what to an infusion of what? Harry glanced at Ron, who looked as stumped as he was; Hermione's hand had shot into the air.*

> *"I don't know, sir," said Harry.*

> *Snape's lips curled into a sneer.*

> *"Tut, tut -- fame clearly isn't everything."*

> *He ignored Hermione's hand.*

> *"Let's try again. Potter, where would you look if I told you to find me a bezoar?"*

Hermione stretched her hand as high into the air as it would go without her leaving her seat, but Harry didn't have the faintest idea what a bezoar was. He tried not to look at Malfoy, Crabbe, and Goyle, who were shaking with laughter.

"I don't know, sir."

"Thought you wouldn't open a book before coming, eh, Potter?"

Harry forced himself to keep looking straight into those cold eyes. He had looked through his books at the Dursleys', but did Snape expect him to remember everything in <u>One Thousand Magical Herbs and Fungi</u>?

Snape was still ignoring Hermione's quivering hand.

"What is the difference, Potter, between monkshood and wolfsbane?"

At this, Hermione stood up, her hand stretching toward the dungeon ceiling.

"I don't know," said Harry quietly. "I think Hermione does, though, why don't you try her?"

A few people laughed; Harry caught Seamus's eye, and Seamus winked. Snape, however, was not pleased.

"Sit down," he snapped at Hermione. "For your information, Potter, asphodel and wormwood make a sleeping potion so powerful it is known as the Draught of Living Death. A bezoar is a stone taken from the stomach of a goat and it will save you from most poisons. As for monkshood and wolfsbane, they are the same plant, which also goes by the name of *aconite...*" [SS-8]

We've certainly seen a bezoar become crucial in our story, when Harry has to save Ron from the poisoned mead in *Half-Blood Prince*. Note Snape not only answers his own question -- where does one *find* a bezoar -- he also tells us what it does: "*...it will save you from most poisons.*" Reading that, we might have thought (in retrospect), "Poisons? Gee, I wonder who in these books is going to get poisoned?"

And wolfsbane also becomes important in *Prisoner of Azkaban* when Lupin the werewolf needs Wolfsbane Potion to deal with his monthly problem. Had we been wearing our set-up/payoff glasses when we first heard Snape ask that question in *Sorcerer's Stone*, we might very well have said to ourselves, "Hm. Wolfsbane, huh? Methinks there'll be a werewolf showing up in this story."

So two of the three items set up in Snape's first class have shown up in crucial ways, ways that amount to saving the lives of the people who receive them. (Cathy Liesner's "Stoppered Death" theory, is, of course, also set up here in Snape's class.)

The only thing we haven't seen from Harry's first Potions class is the Draught of Living Death.

We have been reminded of it, though. In *Half-Blood Prince*, Slughorn has his Advanced Potions students make the Draught of Living Death [HBP-9]. Harry does so perfectly with the help provided in his borrowed Potions book, courtesy of the Half-Blood Prince.

(Note that this constituted a subtle hint as to the identity of the Half-Blood Prince. After all, who was the only person who had previously mentioned the Draught of Living Death? None other than Snape.)

The fact that the Draught is the only thing we saw in that first Potions class that we haven't seen *used*, combined with the fact that we were so pointedly reminded about it (when, face it, Slughorn could have chosen *any* potion to set as an exercise) makes me feel positive we will see it in Book 7.

Some folks thought we *had* seen it already. Many suggested that Dumbledore, rather than being killed by Snape, was actually under the influence of the Draught of Living Death, which indeed causes the imbiber to fall into a deep sleep mimicking death.

However, J.K. Rowling's interview of August 1, 2006 made it explicitly clear that Dumbledore *is* dead.

So we have *not* seen the Draught of Living Death in use. Which means that *someone else* will be the recipient of the Draught of Living Death in Book 7.

I see two major candidates for use of the Draught of Living Death: Snape. Or Harry himself.

Snape has been involved in every other incident involving the ingredients mentioned in that first class. He made the Wolfsbane Potion for Lupin -- a potion so difficult, few are able to make it at all. And it was Snape's notes, as the Half-Blood Prince, that allowed Harry to save Ron's life with the bezoar. So we could reasonably expect to see him involved with the final payoff to that class.

But Harry is also a good candidate. After all, he has now not only learned about the Draught of Living Death from Snape, he has made it under Slughorn's tutelage (with help from the Prince again).

Might there be a point in Book 7 when Harry might wish his enemies to believe him dead? What better way to fool them?

Taking speculation a bit further, what if Harry can't get close enough to Voldemort to attempt to kill him? What if he remembers Dumbledore's words: *"He can't kill you if you're already dead"* [HBP-27]? Mightn't that trigger in Harry an idea: Could he get close to Voldemort if he *were* (effectively) dead?

Rowling is a master of narrative misdirection, after all. What supreme misdirection it would be if Harry were to appear dead, not just to his enemies, not just to Ron and Hermione (imagine their reactions)... but to *us*. (Imagine *our* reactions.)

As John Granger has pointed out in *Looking for God in Harry Potter*, Rowling has put Harry through a pattern of death and resurrection in each book so far. But each time, though we have walked with him to the edge of death, he has not actually died. Wouldn't it be a masterful stroke on Rowling's part to have us believe Harry is dead? A *Romeo and Juliet* moment, if you will, with all the possibilities for misunderstanding and mistaken response that Shakespeare's story held.

Should it happen, it will not be a cheat on her part -- because the set-up is clearly here, waiting for us to recognize it for what it is..

The Draught of Living Death has been waiting six books for its payoff. Since it's taken so long, I'm expecting a terrific payoff indeed.

CHAPTER 33

DRACO THE WOLF-BOY

As we reach the end of my thoughts on set-ups and payoffs, I must say that the concept of this chapter did not originate with me. The idea that Draco could be a werewolf shows up all over the Internet, and I haven't got a clue who originated it. I have, however, given some thought as to how (well) this idea is set up.

Am I convinced Draco has become a werewolf? Not completely. But let's take a look at the evidence.

We first see Draco connected with werewolves in *Sorcerer's Stone,* when he, Harry and Neville have to do detention in the Forbidden Forest with Hagrid. Draco's biggest fear of going into the Forest is werewolves [SS-15]. This moment doesn't necessarily have to be a set-up, but if there's a payoff, then a nice subtle set-up it is.

We also have the non-canonical evidence from the movie of *Prisoner of Azkaban.* While I know too much about how movies are made to take seriously any movie-based clues, nevertheless J.K. Rowling did state that there was *something* in that movie that made her shiver because it was so prescient of a plot point she had not yet revealed. Some people have pointed to the moment when Draco howls like a werewolf in the movie as that instance. Maybe.

The bulk of the clues (if clues they are) about Draco's lycanthropy come, of course, in *Half-Blood Prince.* Let's look at the time line.

We first see Draco in Diagon Alley. He is boastful toward Madam Malkin, won't let her see his left arm [HBP-6], possibly because there is a brand new Dark Mark on it. Draco remains boastful when he takes a detour to Knockturn Alley, where he brags about knowing Fenrir Greyback as if he actually had some control over Fenrir [HBP-6]. We don't know who or what Fenrir is at this point, so while a set-up (or pre-introduction), it doesn't seem that important at the time.

However, we learn later this small moment was indeed important, because Rowling goes out of her way to remind us of it:

> ...[Harry] told [Hermione] all about Lupin's mission among the werewolves and the difficulties he was facing. "Have you heard of this Fenrir Greyback?"
>
> "Yes, I have!" said Hermione, sounding startled. "And so have you, Harry!"
>
> "When, History of Magic? You know full well I never listened..."
>
> "No, no, not History of Magic -- Malfoy threatened Borgin with him!" said Hermione. "Back in Knockturn Alley, don't you remember? He told Borgin that Greyback was an old family friend and that he'd be checking up on Borgin's progress!" [HBP-17]

Note that, if indeed Draco is a werewolf by this point, we're distracted from that possibility by Harry's focus instead on whether Draco is a Death Eater. In a sense, this misdirection makes the set-up even potentially more important: it gives the information we need, but simultaneously points us away from it.

Okay, back to the timeline of Draco's decline.

By mid-October, Draco is in detention for not finishing his Transfiguration homework [HBP-12]. Why? Is he merely distracted by his task of killing Dumbledore, or is there something else distracting him?

In December, Draco misses a Quidditch game due to an unspecified illness, something he's never done before [HBP-14].

Also in December, Harry notices Draco has dark shadows under his eyes, and grayish skin [HBP-15]. Hmm. That description sounds vaguely familiar. Ah yes. As it turns out, Lupin, when recovering from his transformation, is also described as having dark shadows under his eyes [PA-10]. Are Lupin's and Draco's dark shadows for the same reason? Or is Draco just staying up too late?

Draco doesn't get better. In April, he's described as still having that gray skin, and as having lost all his smugness and swagger [HBP-22].

We also learn now that Draco is suffering more than a physical ailment. First we learn a boy has been hiding out in Moaning Myrtle's bathroom. He's been crying, lonely, with no one to talk to, sharing "secrets" with Myrtle [HBP-21]. A few chapters later we learn, surprisingly, that the crying boy is Draco:

> *"No one can help me," said Malfoy. His whole body was shaking. "I can't do it.... I can't.... It won't work... and unless I do it soon... he says he'll kill me....."*

> *And Harry realized, with a shock so huge it seemed to root him to the spot, that Malfoy was crying -- actually crying -- tears streaming down his pale face into the grimy basin.* [HBP-24]

The scene moves from Harry's shock quickly to Harry performing Sectumsempra on Draco -- perhaps distracting us from Draco's "He'll kill me" utterance.

But that utterance is echoed again on the top of the Lightning-Struck Tower:

> "I haven't got any options!" said Malfoy, and he was suddenly white as Dumbledore. "I've got to do it! He'll kill me! He'll kill my whole family!" [HBP-27]

The identity of "he" here is left deliberately ambiguous. We're probably intended to think he's talking about Voldemort. But he could equally be talking about Fenrir Greyback. If so, that initial swagger he showed in boasting about his ties to Fenrir has been replaced by outright fear. Such fear, presumably, has its roots in having seen the terror Fenrir is capable of creating.

Raising the question: Did Draco just *see* that terror? Or did he experience it? Did he actually receive a werewolf bite? (After all, Fenrir likes to bite children, we have learned from Lupin.)

That's the basic evidence for the theory that Draco is now a werewolf. Every bit of it is consistent with Draco having been bitten.... but it is equally consistent with Draco being stressed beyond belief in trying to fulfill the mission set by "him" -- either the Dark Lord, his lieutenant Fenrir, or an evil character to be named later.

We don't know for sure whether or not Draco's a werewolf by the time Snape runs off with him at the end of *Half-Blood Prince*.

Except that Snape sticking with Draco like that could *also* be a set-up to Draco's lycanthropy.

Because let's remember that Snape is one of the few people

who can make the newly-invented Wolfsbane Potion which keeps a werewolf from undergoing his full transformation [PA-18].

We have help remembering this bit of information which we might have thought had lost its usefulness by the end of *Prisoner of Azkaban* -- because, as with the identification of Fenrir Greyback mentioned above, Rowling goes out of her way to remind us of it three books later:

> *"...But I do not forget that during the year I taught at Hogwarts, Severus made the Wolfsbane Potion for me every month, made it perfectly, so that I did not have to suffer as I usually do at the full moon.... We both know he wanted my job, but he could have wreaked much worse damage on me by tampering with the potion. He kept me healthy. I must be grateful."* [HBP-16]

This adds a new significance to Snape protecting Draco and dragging him to safety after the Battle at Hogwarts. Sure, maybe he's just keeping his promise to Narcissa to protect Draco from harm. But really, to keep that promise, would Snape even *need* to remove Draco from Hogwarts? After all, Draco failed to kill Dumbledore. And no one else associated with Hogwarts even knows Draco was on that tower. Wouldn't the safest thing be to shove Draco back in the Slytherin dungeon and tell him to keep his mouth shut?

That might be safest thing were Draco 'normal.' But if Draco *is* a werewolf, to leave him behind at Hogwarts would be the most dangerous thing possible. If Snape is to (continue to?) make the Wolfsbane Potion for Draco, Draco *must* go with him.

...So do I think Draco *is* a werewolf? I'm not fully convinced, but I certainly acknowledge that if he is, the set-ups are there.

I also think that Harry is going to have to forgive Draco before

Book 7 is out -- forgiveness that will more likely take the form of showing pity on him in some active way, something more than standing there making an "I forgive you" speech. And we have consistently seen that when Harry feels pity for someone, he comes closer to being the person he should be, and to letting go of his (and James's and Sirius's) old grudges.

If Draco is a werewolf, it might be much easier for Harry to feel sorry for him.

AFTERWORD

When Charles Dickens was writing his novels in a serialized fashion, the wait for the next installment was just as intense as what we're experiencing now waiting for Book 7 of the *Harry Potter* books. Dickens used to talk about doling out his stories a "teaspoon" at a time. His readers lapped up those teaspoons eagerly, with American readers going so far as to rush to the docks, hoping the next installment had arrived on that day's ship.

In between chapters, the readers would opine loudly as to what had come before (to the point that Dickens even at times incorporated their "notes" into his writing, bringing back popular characters and the like) and would eagerly speculate on what would come next.

Sound familiar?

As I said at the beginning of this book, we are so fortunate to be living suspended between speculation and knowledge. Some time in 2007 J.K. Rowling will publish *Harry Potter and the....* (whatever), and we will know the answers. After that moment, no one will ever again share our current experience.

The danger of speculation is that we become so enamored of our theories that, should Ms. Rowling surprise us (as she undoubtedly will!) we may feel she got it "wrong."

When I read comments to that effect on the Internet, a little ache twinges inside me at the disrespect it shows to this incredibly talented and generous author.

Whatever "answers" we get in Book 7 will be the right answers. However Ms. Rowling chooses to end the story will be the right ending... because it's *her* story first and foremost. I've speculated a lot in this book, always (always!) based on 'canon,' based on what has come before. But where I'm wrong (as I will be in places), I will happily chuck my theory or prediction overboard.

Book 7, after all, isn't the answer key to some giant 3000-plus page test. It's the end of a *story*. I hope we will all be able to forget all our theories and let ourselves be swept along by the story itself.

In the meantime, isn't it fun to speculate?!

Printed in the United States
82643LV00006B/55-57/A